D0410411

Brooklyn
Heights

Brooklyn Heights

Miral al-Tahawy

Translated by
Samah Selim

The American University in Cairo Press
Cairo   New York

First published in 2011 by
The American University in Cairo Press
113 Sharia Kasr el Aini, Cairo, Egypt
420 Fifth Avenue, New York, NY 10018
www.aucpress.com

Dar el Kutub No. 24545/11
ISBN 978 977 416 488 0

Dar el Kutub Cataloging-in-Publication Data

al-Tahawy, Miral
    Brooklyn Heights / Miral al-Tahawy; translated by Samah Selim.—Cairo: The American
University in Cairo Press, 2011
        p.   cm.
        ISBN 978 977 416 488 0
        1. English fiction   I. Title
        823

1 2 3 4 5 6 7 8   14 13 12 11

Designed by Fatiha Bouzidi
Printed in Egypt

Flatbush Avenue

She finds it on a Google map of Brooklyn as she hunts for an apartment, a narrow strip winding its way up to the long arching bridge that connects the two islands. Spanking new cars zoom across the Brooklyn Bridge, pedestrians stream down the walkway, and tourists watch the setting sun from its heights. They gaze in awe at the tip of Manhattan, which looks from up there like a birthday cake ablaze with candles, a round and luscious apple, brilliant with its lit skyscrapers. She turns her back on Manhattan and chooses Flatbush Avenue from among all those myriad streets because it becomes her: a woman shouldering her solitude, a couple of suitcases, and a child who leans into her whenever he grows tired of walking. She carries a few manuscripts of unfinished stories in a small backpack along with the other important documents: birth and vaccination certificates, residence papers, copies of degrees, employers' letters of recommendation, bank papers, and a signed rental contract for an apartment she's never seen.

All she knows is that it's located on the corner of Flatbush and Fifth Avenue near a big public garden in the heart of an old Brooklyn neighborhood called Park Slope. She looks up 'slope' in the dictionary: a rim or bluff—a place of descent. She likes that; somehow it fits. She walks west on Flatbush, which extends from the bridge to the eastern borders of Brooklyn, looking for her building. The avenue stretches out before her long and wide, abruptly intersected by other avenues and streets that twist and turn into different numbers and names. She picks her way along it slowly and carefully because it may well take her into the heart of a world with no pity, because she is afraid most of the time, and because she leads a young child by the hand. She lingers in the peaceful plaza where the smell of children and milky coffee wafts out from cafés and where dark-skinned nannies push baby strollers with one hand and talk into cell phones with the other, their high-pitched laughter drowning out the whimpers of their trapped, squirming charges. The side streets are full of restaurants and cafés that give off an aura of mellow sophistication with their heavy wood furniture and faded oil paintings. She walks down streets that exude an evident passion for everything old, a passion that spills into the aroma of coffee, the gleam of thick-framed spectacles, and the rumble of insomniac scribbling. She watches people sprinting down sidewalks in order to lose a few pounds, people walking elegant and spoiled dogs, people lost in deep plotting of some poem or musical score in the final stages of composition, or perhaps just relaxing before a reiki or yoga session.

She's sure now that she has come to the right place. Everything around her invites nostalgia. She is surrounded by people who seem to be busy with some act of cosmic creation. All of them are writers, as she herself dreams of becoming. They carry backpacks stuffed with hopeful manuscripts. They hunt for agents and publishers and court young magazine editors who will discover their talent by chance and review their work in a few favorable, well-placed lines. And so their dreams come true all at once. She feels at home here in this place where, from a distance at least, people seem to reflect her own image back. She too dreams of writing but her one collection of poems—*I Am Like No Other*—is still a sheaf of loose sheets of paper stowed away in an old white handbag inherited from her mother.

She was dragging the suitcases up to the entrance of the new building when he suddenly stopped and tugged on her hand: "Can I buy something to eat?" Before she could answer, he ran into the store next door and straight up to the man behind the counter (who was of Yemeni origin as they found out later) and said to him with a speed and succinctness in English that astonished her: "A toasted bagel with cream cheese and a strawberry-cranberry juice smoothie." The order sounded as long and wide as Flatbush Avenue. It took her a while to parse out each word. She often had trouble understanding his English in these situations and now she was having trouble counting out the coins whose value she still hadn't memorized. She carefully searched for the right words to make him see sense and ask her first before ordering things they might not be able to afford, but he barely gave her the chance to finish her sentence.

"Darling, what if Mama doesn't have enough money with her?"

"I just ordered a cheese sandwich and a glass of juice, Mom. What's the big deal?" he replied testily. His sharp retort reduced her to silence, and the bitter memory of the bagel 'incident' stayed with her for a long time after. Flatbush Avenue was full of temptations.

The apartment they moved into was not sized to fit his dreams either. It was no bigger than a small matchbox with a window looking out onto the street. Later she kept trying to convince him that she had chosen the nicest view of Brooklyn just for him. She told him that he could wave to the nice Mr Falafel from the window, who was in the habit of sitting outside his restaurant on a large chair between two life-sized painted wooden statues of King Tutankhamun and Queen Nefertiti. He would carry the two statues outside in the morning to welcome his customers and she would watch him take them back inside in the evening when he shut up shop. Of course neither she nor her son ever dared to pass between those statues because Mr. Falafel sold his sandwiches at ten dollars apiece. They contented themselves with watching him open and close from their window on the third floor and smiling at him as he sat between his royal friends.

A small, dingy Chinese restaurant called Tofu stood next to Mr. Falafel. It was an especially unpleasant meal. They sat for a long time at a rickety table and drank glasses of water from a tin pitcher carelessly placed in front of them. As always she listened as her son sped through his complicated order. His aptitude with menus no longer amazed her. She only watched him as he pronounced the words quickly and with mystifying confidence: "Vegetarian noodles with black mushrooms and zucchini." She nodded to the waiter in confirmation. The strange words came piled up in a large bowl that he dug into irritably, after drenching the contents with soy sauce. She was foolish enough to open up one of the oddly shaped biscuits that came in a small clear plastic wrapper and bite into its brittle, tasteless crust. She spat it out quickly.

"What is this?"

The boy giggled furiously. "You're not supposed to eat it, Mom. You're just supposed to read the fortune inside."

She was ever eager to read her fortune in anything and everything: horoscopes, tarot and playing cards, sometimes her palm. Her forehead was also a possibility, if she could have found someone who knew how to interpret its mysterious lines, but she would never have thought to discover it written out on a tiny piece of paper rolled up into a minute scroll. She opened it up with the trepidation of those who approach the inexorable destiny inscribed in print. *That which awaits you is no better than that which you have left behind.* She tore up the paper into tiny bits and threw them into her glass of water. She got up to leave, and he hurried out behind her.

"Mom, are you angry with me? Did I spend a lot of money, Mom? Are you mad?"

She kept walking and he ran after her in the direction of the small box that was now their home.

At night she thinks about how she has begun to forget so many things—addresses, events, the whereabouts of documents. She worries that her keen memory is getting moldy. She, who once believed that forgetting was a great blessing, is now hunted by oblivion, a monstrous shadow.

She tries to remember the shape of other houses that she has lived in and fails. She knows that she now lives in a house that gathers all streets into itself, a house like a glass box. People look in and see her, she looks out and sees them, jogging, drinking, embracing their lovers. It is a house that confirms her solitude and verifies her talent for escaping. She often takes long walks along Flatbush Avenue. She studies the places where others have lived and tries to chart a map with which to replace the memories she has fled, the memories that have left a blank space in their wake.

Lefferts Historic House is close to the street where they live. She discovers that long ago, a wealthy Irish landowner by the name of Mr. Busch once owned the entire street and all the houses on it. She takes her son by the hand and they go inside. The mansion has been preserved in its original state. It has a large garden that borders Prospect Park. Together they examine the ground water pump, the tea room and the upper-story bedrooms, the fireplace, and the walls covered with portraits of the owner and his children, their servants and slaves standing behind them in the shadows, polishing the wood floors and pouring tea from silver pots. The servants slept there, in the stables, on piles of straw that have been carefully recreated for visitors.

She inspects a few antique paintings of Brooklyn in the days when it was an island of farmers and a harbor for docking ships: barns full of straw, vast farms, and open fields strewn with the ruins of deserted vessels. If she walks out from the museum, crosses the park, and makes her way to the warren of narrow streets that they call Fort Greene—home to the largest community of African-Americans in Brooklyn—she will see dark-skinned women sitting on their stoops and chatting together in shrill voices, though she won't understand a word of what they are saying in between the deep-throated laughter that sounds much like her own. They speak at breakneck speed and puff on cigarettes to the strains of loud music coming through the open windows—music that drifts through a neighborhood rich with the African caftans, chili and spices, oils and perfumes, and colorful jewelry of the hot, brown continent that is also hers. Night falls on Fort Greene and she can hear the sound of exploding fireworks and popping balloons and shouts full of sudden, cataclysmic enthusiasm. A deep chant rumbles along the length of Flatbush Avenue and wakes it from its slumber. She opens her window, laughing out loud and clapping her hands like a madwoman. Hundreds of people open their windows to watch the fireworks and those funny balloons with images of Obama stamped on them floating in from sleepless Red Hook. After the fireworks, people stream out onto the streets waving old maps of Brooklyn in the days before the great bridge was built. In those days the neighborhood was made up of small wretched shacks occupied by freed slaves and poor whites looking for work in the iron foundries and glass factories or working as day laborers in the fields. The big blue signs have been visible everywhere on the avenues and streets since her arrival: *Change*. She pins a button printed with that word on her chest as a token of her own soon-to-be-fulfilled dreams. Her son has the same button pinned to his school bag. They wear them because like everyone else they too crave change, and its sister declaration: *Hope*; words that make them feel that they have become a part of this map, a part of its deepest aspirations. Her son emerged from under the blankets and opened his eyes wide.

"What's going on?"

"Obama won."

He smiled, then closed his eyes and went back to sleep while she stayed at the window watching the fireworks, the joy, then the fatigue, then the light of dawn breaking on the avenue littered with empty beer bottles. She listened to the noise made by the giant street cleaning trucks, then the pregnant silence that rose with the sun. A bit later the express bus to Manhattan passed under her window. She watched the office workers hurrying to the subway station and breathed in the aroma of coffee drifting out of apartment windows and cafés and doughnut vans. Later that morning he tapped her on the shoulder and asked her the same question again.

"Did Obama really win, Mom?"

"Yes."

He trots after her from the small bedroom to the even smaller kitchen and begins to tick off his laundry list of Obama-inspired wishes. She faces him with a grave expression and gives him her undivided attention because he often complains that she ignores him. She nods her head and restricts herself to a single word, 'yes,' a word he has grown to hate, a meaningless word conveying nothing, but it's the only one she's got these days.

"I've got to tell Obama that a lot of things have to change."

"Okay."

The boy picked out his English words with care. "He has to change the *environment* and the *rain forest* and *go green everywhere* and change Egypt too. Can he do that?"

"Let's hope so. Everything will turn green."

"Can I be in an election and win like Obama?"

"Anything is possible."

"And be the president of the *United States?*"

"Anything is possible."

"Now? *Now?*"

"There's a time and place for everything, my love."

She feels like she's getting old. She realizes that she has been repeating the same resigned, cautious, and ultimately meaningless words her own mother used ad nauseam ("God willing. . . . It's all up to Him. . . . Who knows? . . . There's a time and place for everything. . . .") and that she's beginning to resemble her mother more and more as time goes by, especially after she cut off the long coal-black hair that now smells of her mother's favorite Japanese dye. Her walk has also taken on the same listless gait that her mother had at the end of a long day; her mother who constantly brandished her dictionary of essential and incontrovertible truths in order to shackle Hend's dreams of becoming an airline hostess, or an astronomer. "All knowledge belongs to God, dear, and He commands all," she would laughingly instruct. So she lets the boy write a long letter to Obama. She remembers that she used to write long letters to her

God. He never once replied of course but that didn't stop her from believing that He would make all her dreams come true.

She takes him by the hand and walks. She walks and walks because today is her day off and because the apartment she lives in is stifling and because she can't sleep at night and because her buried anxiety gives the placid expression in her eyes a frightening cast. When they come home at the end of the day he will lie next to her and watch TV and she'll bury her head even deeper under the covers and dream about them; about the life that she can no longer remember, the life that is slipping through her hands.

Her name is Hend but her nicknames were many. She remembers certain ones: 'Gap-tooth' when her milk teeth were falling out, 'Bucky' because of her protruding upper jaw, 'Thumbs' because her hands weren't able to grasp things properly, as hands should. Objects would slip away from her and shatter because her mind was always far away. Those cruel names turned her into an obstinate mule and made her relationship with her mother a living hell. She would brush her hot tears away with a final sob before exploding into the same insistent stream of questions: "Why don't you love me? Are you really my mother?" Sometimes her anger drove her to excess: "I hate you, I hate you!" she would scream. Someone would usually intervene at this point to teach her better manners and she always emerged from the subsequent battle with a brand new set of wounds.

She was never able to beat a prudent retreat from these battles. Her childish insolence and the feeble scratches she meted out were met with a few fierce slaps that made her long, crooked nose bleed. She would run away to hide under the low wooden bed and cry bitter tears. After a while she would stifle her sobs to listen for the approaching click of those dainty feather slippers that she so coveted. From her spot under the bed, she glimpsed a shiny red heel and the hem of her mother's lace nightgown. Night would have fallen by now. The smell of her father's cigarette wafts in from the room next door. After drawn-out negotiations, she emerges from under the bed. The mother reaches out her arm to smooth the daughter's hair and to draw her close, but the daughter resists. "Come here, princess, come to me." Hend gnaws her lip and brushes away the last traces of her tears. "You don't love me," she whimpers. Her mother hugs her tight. "Are you crazy? How can a mother not love her daughter? You're the most precious thing in the world to me." In a flash of clarity, those wistful words reveal to Hend the true extent of their shared despair.

In spite of all of the attempts to break her in, Hend never managed to become the gentle and obedient girl capable of thriving in a jungle of men that her mother hoped and prayed she would become. All the meticulous and chary instructions—"You're a girl, how will you manage to survive with that stubborn head of yours?"— didn't do a bit of good. After all those years, after learning the meaning of suspicion and jealousy and desertion, she now understood that the woman forever pacing the living room in a honey-colored robe was her twin. They both had the same long nose, worn down by endless nights of crying. She recalled her mother's habit of clutching at her lower back to soothe the chronic pain left behind by many childbirths. She would apply one hot water bottle after another to still the ache while she waited long into the night for Hend's father to come home—if he bothered to come home at all. She refused to believe the many stories that the servants told her about her husband, and the dark circles under her bloodshot eyes told a story of their own in the morning.

Hend knew that if her mother woke up in one of those states a domestic volcano was sure to erupt and that, as the only daughter, she would be its main victim. She would scurry back to her place under the bed yet again, whimpering and listening for the torrent of threats to smash in her stubborn head. She wasn't an entirely innocent party in these battles, for she was more than capable of challenging her mother with her defiant, intimidating eyes. She was also quite good at singlehandedly provoking her anger by poking through her private things—her makeup cases and bits of paper carefully shut away in drawers, like the clippings that her mother collected from *Your Personal Doctor* and *Eve*, and a host of other magazines specializing in domestic and marital problems. There were articles about how to monopolize your husband's love by putting perfume in your bathwater and sweet-smelling mastic in the folds of your underwear, or how to make sticky caramelized sugar paste to remove unattractive body hair. She devoured all this in an excess of curiosity, not paying the slightest attention to her mother's warnings. The only thing that saved her from her mother's wrath was that she was a model student. Hend's mother took comfort in the hope that her daughter would make something of herself someday, perhaps by getting a higher education. In the meantime she didn't bother to hide her anxiety about Hend's future and would often remind her that she was not pretty and therefore shouldn't count on her looks to get her through life. It didn't help that she was no good at housekeeping and so God only knew who would be willing to marry her.

Hend was in fact married for a few years. She had a baby, she sprinkled perfume on her pillowcases, she kept her supple skin smooth and inviting. She diligently followed all the instructions that she had pored over as a young girl, such as "how to ward off marital boredom and keep your husband by frequently changing the color of your underwear" and "learning the difference between acceptable and unacceptable jealousy." But all of these recipes led to the same dead end that her mother had predicted a long time before. The simple fact was that she was 'no good,' and that she didn't understand the first thing about life or men.

The history of that short-lived marriage was summed up in an endless string of domestic spats involving slamming doors and hurtful expressions like "I never loved you," "If you don't like it, there's the door," "You're disgusting . . . you're a fool!" These verbal skirmishes evolved soon enough into packed suitcases and copious tears and neighbors spying and friends intervening. That was when a simple truth, clear as the light of day, gradually dawned on her: one of them had to choose the best way out.

One morning, her husband took a shower, splashed on his favorite cologne, carefully chose a pair of white cotton underwear still soft and velvety like a first night of passion, stuffed a pair of black silk pajamas and some condoms into his briefcase, then walked out the door and never came back. A few months later, Hend put everything that still belonged to her into a few suitcases, covered the furniture in plastic sheeting, and left with her bags in tow. From her husband she inherited a visa for the US, a child, and two suitcases containing the smallest and lightest of his toys. And this was how they ended up in a tiny apartment on the corner of Flatbush and Fifth. Her father used to say, "Whatever the north wind brings, the south wind takes away." And here she stands now, wretched and alone, in a place where the four winds mightily converge. The women around her—some younger, most older—who come from all over God's mysterious lands look exactly like herself in ways that are painful, frightening, and comforting at the same time. Every day she crosses Grand Army Plaza to go to the subway station or the public library. She likes to go to the library to look at the pictures of famous writers whose ranks she dreams of joining. They comfort her high up there on the walls, because they, like her, one day discovered that life is not beautiful. She moves past Hemingway's portrait and shyly sits down next to some people who seem much more at ease than herself. Above the table there is a poster with the words "Learn English" printed on it. Next to the poster hangs a black and white photograph of Albert Einstein, underneath which is written, "Einstein was a refugee too."

My name is Hend. I came here from Cairo—why, I don't exactly know. I'm trying to learn English. I love the Arabic language. I used to be an Arabic teacher. I feel really shy whenever I have to speak in English. Even the words I've learned properly I seem to pronounce in a way that no one can understand. I like to go to places where cultured people gather, and I pretend to be one of them though I don't really understand what they are talking about. I sit on a chair in a far corner so that no one bothers to ask me anything and I don't feel the need to say anything. The expression, "Excuse me, what did you say?" which I hear all the time, makes me freeze. I have a serious problem communicating with people. I know that Pluto is in the House of Capricorn—meaning in the seventh house opposite Cancer. This is the house of tolerance and compassion. Maybe that's the reason people don't understand me—because the opposing energy of Pluto is facing my zodiac sign. I feel my stupidity and ignorance more than at any other time in my life. I feel that I have to rethink so many things.

The others introduce themselves simply and clearly.

"Fatima from Mali. Twenty-four years old. I grew up in France. I came here to visit family. I'm a salesgirl in a store."

"Emilia. I came from Russia with my husband twenty years ago. I'm really old! I don't even know how old I am any more. I'd like to find someone to talk to."

"Faridnaz, Pakistan. Twenty-two. Recently married. I came here to join my husband."

"Alejandro from Peru. I'm a building superintendent."

"Nazahat. I'm from Bosnia. I used to be a doctor. I'm fifty-five."

"My name is Dawij. I come from Haiti. I'm eighteen years old. I clean houses."

"Said. My name is Said. I'm an Egyptian Copt. I'm a limousine driver."

They always change. Some come and some vacate their places for new ones to come. After class, they peddle cosmetics and cleaning detergents. The informal introductions are always much simpler. With her they exchange truncated sentences, as though she were an outsider, not belonging. Some of them ask her in bad Arabic: "Is you Muslim?" She nods her head happily, longing for connection, a few friendships or acquaintances to pass into her life. She talks about her country and tries to pinpoint its location for them somewhere between Israel and Mecca—those two poles of strategic interest in the region. She is forced to show her own ignorance when she asks about the location of Haiti or Peru. In the end, they exchange the useful tidbits of information gleaned by exiles and immigrants: the best places to shop cheaply, job openings, where to find soup kitchens and welfare offices, rental prices for apartments or single rooms, and short, cheap excursions to places like Sheepshead Bay near the end of the subway line where the exiles sit on benches by the sea that reminds them of other ports and waterways. They spend the endless time on their hands fishing in the ocean that separates them from their homelands. They watch the passing ships and gaze at the Statue of Liberty in the distance, the Verrazano Bridge, and the contours of New Jersey. They smoke cigarettes and talk about the motherland and things like visas and health insurance and social security.

In class she gets to know a lot of Arabs who have recently arrived from Morocco and Algeria, Sudan and Yemen. They never speak to her in Arabic: "I speak colloquial," they say, if she tries to draw them into conversation. They chatter together in bad English and claim that they know next to nothing about each others' countries because the Arab world is so big and wide and very different. She tries to believe this, and she tells them that she's an Arabic teacher, that Arabic is an endangered language, a language that is slowly dying out, but she clings to it because unfortunately, she tends to get insanely attached to things and love defies forgetfulness.

She clutches her papers and crosses Flatbush, talking to herself. She often talks to herself in that obscure, whispered, endangered language that makes passersby stare at her. She sits on the wooden bench in front of her son's school, sipping coffee, smoking a cigarette, and waiting for him to come out. The cold pierces her to the bone and the cigarette doesn't warm her up. She muses on the cold piling up in layers around her face, turning her into a tired, autumnal woman, a woman naked and alone who resembles no one. He comes toward her slowly, gingerly, and he doesn't kiss her. He gently puts his hand in her hand and they walk side by side, keeping pace. Mother and son are almost the same height. He startles her with questions to which she has no answers.

"Mom, you didn't do your hair."

"What do you mean?"

"You look strange these days. Why don't you put makeup on any more?"

"Maybe I don't have time."

"You just don't care how you look."

"The important thing is that I care about you. What did you do today?"

"We had a demonstration and we made signs saying *Change*, and we had a food strike."

"Why?"

"The food in the school cafeteria is awful. Every day it's the same thing. So we all complained and we wrote a letter saying that we want pizza and hamburgers and ice cream instead, and we waved pictures of Obama with 'Change' written on them. You have to change too, Mom."

"How?"

"Your hair, for example. The way you look. You know. . . ."

"So you don't like your mother any more?"

"No, it's just that you have to change. You're always sad. *Sad*," he repeated in English.

"Okay."

"But Mom?"

"Yes?"

"When you change the way you dress and everything, you have to promise me that you won't love anyone else. You can go out with your friends and have fun—you know, you can *hang out* with them."

"Fine."

"But if one of your friends asks you to go out on a *date*, you have to say no. *Date* means you have to get married and stuff, and I don't want you to love anyone else."

"Fine."

"I'll always keep on loving you, but in *high school* I might start doing dates and go out with a *girlfriend*!"

"Okay, when we get to high school we'll figure it out."

"But I'll never ever leave you, and I'll always visit you. You can even live with me when you get old and stuff."

"Of course. I'll get old and wrinkly and die."

"But I don't want you to get old."

". . ."

"Or die."

"All right then, I won't."

Bay Ridge

Flatbush Avenue is crossed by many streets, like Fifth Avenue, where she now lives. She travels the vast length of Flatbush alone because for the longest time she was too shy to go into any of the many Arab cafés and restaurants by herself. She takes him by the hand and walks along the boardwalk, watching the small ferries crossing the Narrows. She walks till she can no longer feel her feet moving. She wants to get rid of those extra pounds and the din of the thoughts crowding and jostling in her head.

"I know this street by heart," he says in a thin, irritable voice. "I don't want to go to Bay Ridge again. *Please.*"

She can't leave him at home by himself and he can't keep up with her long, hurried strides for miles on end. Sometimes he insists on staying home: "I don't want to go to Bay Ridge!" And when he does go with her, the sacrifice is inevitably tied to a long list of demands: "If I go with you, can I . . . ? Can I buy . . . ? Can I have . . . ?" The older he gets, the more he reminds her of his father. The older he gets, the more she begins to realize that they are each moving in opposite directions, and that she will have to let go soon.

On her way to Bay Ridge, she passes through many different ethnic neighborhoods. There's the Mexican area, where doors are never shut fast and people sell homemade ice-cold drinks from hospitable stoops. The women have skin the color of wheat and thick black hair like her own. They cross the threshold of middle age in bright colorful clothing that bares their full, sated breasts. Playing children dart and weave around them. She watches the unemployed day laborers standing in groups on the wide sidewalks, waiting for work with tool kits in hand—ropes, bits of iron, small axes, garden shears. Rough hands and sturdy muscles ready to carry and move and fix just about anything. They look a lot like the day laborers she used to see scattered in squares and on the narrow sidewalks of her own country. They too wait patiently for small jobs that may or may not materialize. They sit here and there in circles, rubbing their rough hands in slow, relaxed, almost ritual motions, sharing cigarettes and coffee and cheap street food, staring down the unknown with fierce, defiant eyes. She's afraid of these gatherings, which are always pregnant with the possibility of sudden, mysterious fights breaking out, trivial skirmishes with passersby, or conspiratorial whispers that end in heckling a passing woman like herself with the short dark hair of their sisters, and a child in tow.

On her walk she passes the cemetery that sits on top of a hill and looks down upon a huge church. She is fond of the plaster virgins that stand in front of the houses of this neighborhood. She feels that she herself is frozen, like them, in some dimension or other, with that same expression of martyrdom. She likes the atmosphere of the cemetery and the colorful bouquets of plastic flowers. She likes to see the old women sitting in rocking chairs on their porches. Their friendly greetings always take her by surprise. The Latino neighborhood is much gayer. Beautiful mulatto women noisily bustle around houses whose front rooms have been turned into small restaurants. In the evening many of them are transformed into schools or dance halls for salsa and tango. The smell of the great trade in temporary joy wafts out from around them: music, warm bars, the dancers vying in the talent for speed, and the scent of intoxicating green smoke drifts through the places of buying and selling.

She's never had the chance to linger into the night there. He always pulls at her clothes to drag her away as though in fear of the spectacle of bodies coming close together in the dance. He would pull her by the hand in the direction of the bus stop, then begin his interrogation.

"Mom, do you love me?"

"Of course."

"And you'll never leave me?"

"Never."

"Okay, let's go home."

Her father's house was like no other house. As a child, Hend would wander around the village and peer at the dark clay houses that opened onto long corridors and narrow alleys. Their roofs were made of straw piled in high mounds and the walls were left unpainted. Through the open doors she could see interior court-yards and cowsheds, or large ceramic urns and clay braziers with a teapot or a few potatoes perched in their smoky bellies. On cold nights, cats—and sometimes people—would climb up to sleep on the warm stone ledges of these ovens. The doors of all the houses around stood open to her gaze. On her walk, she could see all their nooks and crannies: the plastic bamboo mats for sitting and sleeping, the noisy play of children, men and women gathered in the rituals of dispute and forgiveness.

The streets were dry and dusty in the summer and full of sticky mud in the winter. She walked along them on her daily trip to the mosque and she watched the women pour the dirty washing water out in front of their houses. The smell of cooking wafted out from kerosene stoves, and the smell of dung and laundry detergent filled the air. In the mosque's interior courtyard she contemplated the tall eucalyptus tree that stood next to the wooden bier on which the dead were washed in preparation for burial. She passed the power station, the municipal registry of births, and the local threshing machine. She heard the loud rhythmic sound of the gears grinding in its guts, and the clamor of the women crowding around it. She passed the village's only public drinking water faucet fixed above its stone basin. On her way to the Muqawi Primary School, she saw lots of things.

She is certain now that their house was not like any of the other houses. Her father's house was surrounded by a sturdy mud wall covered with colored chalk pictures of camels, litters, and caravans traveling to Mecca with drawn curtains. The drawings, smudged now by rain, were a record of her family's descent from a tribe of grandfathers whose ancestors bestowed the precious linen cloth from the Land of the Copts upon the sacred Ka'ba. They were meant to bear witness to the long-ago voyage of a pilgrim who had saddled his camels, gathered his men, and ridden the sea to cross over to those blessed shores, and then safely return from the land of God's chosen Prophet. In the middle of the wall stood a huge gate, once stately and imposing but now battered by time and patched up with wooden planks. Inside the walls, an avenue of eucalyptus and flame trees led to a number of small, adjoining clay rooms. An old Cadillac inhabited one of them and the others were all empty like abandoned train cars. The grandfather's wives were once housed in those rooms—the purebred Arab Bedouin woman, the noblewoman descended from the Prophet's line, and the Coptic wife. Her father inherited these structures, like everything else, from his father, and the empty clay rooms were eventually used to store grain and feed. It was the ideal spot for games of hide and seek. Her mother sent the children to play there whenever guests came to visit.

Their house was not beautiful. A flight of steps ascended to a large balcony that led in turn to a vast, bare reception room, empty of furniture because "furniture is so easily broken." The mother would spread a rush mat on the floor in the summer and a woven wool carpet in the winter. In this wide-open space the children ate and ran around and did battle. With the seasons the family moved from the western balcony to the eastern balcony and from the summer room to the winter room. The reception room was normally reserved for guests, and the door to the father's room was always shut fast.

The mother sits in the balcony and dreams of a new house like the many-storied houses of the village with commanding views of the world inside and out. The mother plucks up her courage and tells the father of her dreams: "I wish I could live in a house like that of my noble uncle Lamlum." The father, who has just taken the last sip of his bottle of beer, will twirl his mustache ironically and reply, "God bless him, my dear. He's the son of Bedouins just like us—or was he born with the mark of prophecy on his shoulder?" Her mother, who usually avoids talking about her distant uncles, will turn her face away from him in silent anger. Just once, upon the death of the uncle in question, she took Hend with her on a trip to that faraway house. Her mother spent half that memorable day washing, ironing, and brushing her black mourning clothes, and rummaging through her remaining jewels and perfumed handkerchiefs in musty drawers. In a picture-perfect image, like a photograph preserved in an old family album, she turns to adjust her husband's tie as Hend stands there watching them in her crisp blue dress and shiny white ribbons.

The old Cadillac carries them through vast expanses of sandy land on the edges of Buheira Province. Hend's grandmother, the Sharifa, is very fat and white. She places a pinch of snuff in her nostrils and sneezes into an embroidered white handkerchief. She wipes away the tears with real feeling, shaking her head in a movement that signifies her resignation to God's will. Hend's mother sits opposite her, stiff and elegant, and cries a little. She exchanges kisses with young women dressed in black, plunged in conversation on subjects near and far. The mother's nose colors slightly as she carefully inspects the jewelry, the elegant clothes, the sheer stockings, and the brass coffeepots around her, and inhales the pungent smell of Meccan incense perfuming the air. She finishes her cup of coffee, kisses the hand of the noble grandmother with deliberate emotion, and takes her leave. For a long time after this visit, the father will avoid upsetting her. When she boasts about her dead aristocratic uncles, he will reply with feeling, "God have mercy on us all."

Their house was not many-storied as the mother fervently wished it to be. The floor of the eastern balcony was covered in polished black and white tiles like a chess board. Hend drew a hopscotch course on it with chalk. Sometimes the children used it to mark out opposing goalposts for soccer matches or invisible corners for hide-and-seek and games of 'blind bear.' A heavy door inlaid with a pair of stained-glass windows stood in the middle of the house. The cracked glass panels were crisscrossed with tracks of white soldering glue. The door was very heavy and difficult to open and close. It was repeatedly subjected to fierce slams that inevitably produced more cracks in the glass. The delicate colored glass tended to break into pieces whenever an angry hand happened to fall upon it; her father's hand in particular would make it shudder and splinter whenever he slammed it behind him, cursing the wretched day on which he was born. Afterward, Hend would discover her mother curled up tight into a shaking, weeping ball.

Other kinds of tremors often assailed that unfortunate door: the shrill shouts of playing children running to catch balls that invariably overshot their mark and crashed into the glass. Each of the five boys had left his mark on the walls and windows of the chaotic house, as they had done on their besieged mother's body. Her father's room, however, was the exception to the rule. It was always quiet and tidy. No one dared to open its door unless the father was stretched out on his bed, reading the papers, his wife sitting on a chair at his side in her sesame- and honey-colored robe printed with red flowers, talking calmly. Hend would be playing somewhere or other, her ear cocked to catch the tone of his voice. If it was clear and full of laughter, spring would come to caress their glass door. Mother smiled happily and didn't scold, even when Hend covered her face in flour to scare her brothers, or climbed all the way up the flame tree in a monkey-jump contest, or poured a whole bottle of lavender cologne on her chest before poking through the powders and lotions in her mother's drawers.

Hend runs happily through the house. She collects handfuls of sandy earth and stones and bits of old toys and empty bottles and plays her favorite game—'little house.' On the dusty ground she draws the outlines of a house, with kitchens and children. She puts the rag doll on her lap and feeds it milk from her breast. She sweeps the corners of her imaginary house, a house whose windows are always caressed by spring, a house in which she drifts off to sleep untroubled by the dark shadow of a man shouting at a woman dressed in a robe the color of honey and sesame seeds: "I'll go to hell and you'll never see me again! Do you think you can tie me down with a pile of children?" In other nightmares she sees him dragging the woman along by the embroidered border of her honey-colored robe. In this dream he says to her: "Get out! That's it. I don't want you any more!"

Hend knew that the heavy thud of groans and kicks coming from behind the door would surely shatter its colored glass panels. Her mother always emerged from these battles with exhausted, swollen eyes. The next morning she bound the door's wounds with plastic strips to stop the cold winter wind from coming in through the cracks.

The gate of her father's house was huge and ancient. One day, long ago, the camel caravans went out through that door and never came back. She contemplates it from the inside. She ponders the movement of the universe from behind it. The gaiety of passersby, the screams of children she doesn't know, a ball made of stuffed socks that passes between the nimble feet of running boys. In spite of the threats she opens it cautiously, or creeps underneath it. She steals glances at the girls who look nothing like her. They play out there, on open ground. One of her brothers will pull her away by her hair if he sees her dawdling outside. Her mother says to her, "I'll break your legs if you cross the threshold." So she looks at the dividing line and swallows her want till the day when she too can step over to the other side and never come back.

Hend watches the gypsies pass through in springtime. They stream by in front of the gate and their animals kick up a cloud of dust behind them. She wanders in the space behind their tents pitched on the banks of the Abbasiya Canal. She dreams of a house that hugs the street to itself, a house whose insides she can see without having to knock, a house with a wide hospitable courtyard that invites the greetings of passersby, a house across whose open threshold floats the smell of cooking, of washing, and of the sweat of strangers. But the gate of her father's house is high and shut fast. She stands staring at it and it stares back at her.

Now Hend walks along the endless streets of Brooklyn. She never gets tired of walking in this land, alone and anonymous. She passes through Latino and Italian neighborhoods and arrives in the Asian neighborhood where she likes to shop for fruit and vegetables. She compares prices in the cheaper Vietnamese markets. She passes through the Turkish neighborhood and continues on to Bay Ridge. She is amazed at how the architecture, the people's faces and their skin color, the merchandise and the wafting cooking smells are all so different. By now she will have walked for more than seventy blocks. By now she will have grown weary of the cacophony of languages and loud music and she will begin to long for the sweet aroma of water pipes. She heads for a small local coffeehouse. The men inside flash curious smiles at her. Their good-natured dirty jokes remind her of home. Here is the Arab world in microcosm—the Brooklyn Gulf. They come from Gaza and Nablus, Beirut and Alexandria. The old men of the first generation stretch out in their wooden chairs and curse their exile as they nibble on sweet Arab pastries from The Groom's Sweets next door. Through the window she watches old men come in and out of the storefronts: Seaside Fish, Abu Ali's Falafel, Friendship Kushari, and Abu Kamal's Grocery, which sells halal meat. Old photographs hang in the windows of the Arab shops as well as maps of antique cities and signs proclaiming solidarity with the suffering people of Gaza and southern Lebanon. The residents spill joyfully out onto the streets when Egypt beats Brazil in a soccer match, even if the team hasn't qualified for the World Cup. They pour insults on FIFA in a myriad of dialects.

The coffeehouse she likes to go to is called The Arabian Nights. It's small and dark and the tobacco pipes smell of stale water. The first time she steps inside, she sniffs the air slowly and cautiously.

She glances around her stealthily and realizes that she's the only woman in the place so she sits down and starts leafing through some newspapers and yellowed magazines. The waiter is tall and skinny. He reminds her of her Arabic language teachers back home. The clients call him "sir" out of affection but also, as she discovers later, as a mark of respect for his mysterious past. She tries to hide her face behind the newspaper but he accosts her with the same pointed question:

"Do you live alone?"

"Yes."

"Have you found a job yet?"

"Luckily, yes."

"So I guess you have a visa."

"I have a residence permit."

"You mean a green card?"

"No. I'm a schoolteacher."

She is lying, and he keeps asking her questions she doesn't know how to answer. In Bay Ridge, they kill the heavy time on their hands by inventing ingenious questions designed to expose the white lies of newcomers; immigrants like them looking for a visa, a job, and a room. Muhammad, the waiter, continues:

"What do you teach?"

"Arabic."

"You think Arabs in America need to learn Arabic? Now they're bringing teachers over here?"

" . . ."

"So you're working?"

"I've got papers."

"Does it put bread on the table?"

"Sometimes."

"Look, consider me a brother. Forget the visa and the teaching and all that stuff. If you need a job just say so. I'll be right here. I've been here for fourteen years."

"All right."

"I've got a B.A. in business administration. I used to dream of being a merchant sailor. You see what I do now."

"Yes, I can see."

"You don't like to talk much. It's obvious."

She nods her head slightly and says, "Sometimes."

He looks like he's finally on the point of giving up. He is puzzled by this woman who comes by herself and leaves by herself and seems to be afraid of opening up, talking about any old thing or making up stories, like the others do to give their lives some meaning.

"Okay then," he says glumly, "if you need something just holler."

"Thanks," she answers curtly, which seems to annoy him even more.

She watches the marijuana smoke spiraling up and wreathing the TV screen, which is showing a soccer match. The game draws a slew of crude comments: your mother, your sister, the whore that you married, any old excuse for exchanging friendly insults. A man comes up and introduces himself, and takes a seat at her table as he munches on a piece of sweet pastry. From his accent she can tell that he is from Iraq. He tells her that he was the first of the lot to arrive in Bay Ridge but that he can't quite remember the exact number of years. He wipes away a piece of kunafa stuck to his lip and his sharp, thin smile makes him look like an eagle just before it swoops down on its prey. The deep purple circles under his eyes make her wonder whether he might be an alcoholic despite his constant chatter about the Islamic Center on the corner of Fulton Street and MacDougal. He questions her in the same familiar and slightly suspicious tone as Muhammad the waiter:

"Are you married?"

She shakes her head ambiguously, so he launches into the second question.

"Do you have children?"

"A boy," she replies.

Abd al-Karim is a Kurd, and he seems nicer than he looks. He smiles again and starts to give her advice. "Children are the most important thing in the world. Life here is hard. You have to keep a constant eye on your kids."

He finally gets up and goes back to his interrupted game of dominoes. Later, when she has gotten to know the café and its clients a bit better, she learns that Abd al-Karim was part of the first waves of refugees to come from Iraq and that he married a Mexican girl called Jojo. Jojo used to work in a coffeeshop in Brighton Beach. She was dark-skinned and voluptuous, all silky flesh and curves, made for love. Hend wonders whether Abd al-Karim himself, with his thick mustache and his unusual tallness, used to be attractive in some long-ago time. The couple rented a small apartment in Brighton Beach because Jojo felt more comfortable living in a mixed Russian and Italian neighborhood rather than an Arab one. She admitted this frankly to Hend. She loved the ocean, the cozy local bars, the stout Russian men who looked a little like her husband. She claimed that their tough exteriors hid big hearts—men who turn into fragile, suffering creatures after their first drink. She confessed to Hend that she had had affairs while Abd al-Karim was out driving his taxi day and night, and she would complain bitterly about the strong smell of arak that always clung to her ex-husband. She left him pretty quickly after their third daughter was born, but he didn't move out because he didn't have anyplace else to go. Besides, he wanted to stay close to the girls, who were growing up quickly. He watched this happen with mounting anxiety. His oldest daughter, Diana, was beginning to look just like her mother, slender, voluptuous, and alluring, the exquisite fruit of mixed parentage. She took after her mother in many ways. She was shameless and defiant and full of teeming life. She was also brutally honest to the point of insolence. No one but her Creator could control her, as Abd al-Karim was in the habit of saying. She had inherited the hated dark circles under his eyes and she waged constant war on them with concealers and creams. Like her mother, she was obsessed with the arts of the body—massage therapy, moisturizers, and face masks—and she loved being photographed in provocative poses. Abd al-Karim beat her ferociously sometimes, or else he smashed the furniture in the apartment, and picked fights for the most trivial reasons. After these fits, Jojo always kicked him out of the house and filed restraining orders with the police. He would have ended up in jail on a number of occasions if not for the intervention of the people at the Islamic Center, who patiently talked to him about cultural differences and did the best they could to put out the fire burning in his heart.

He finally moved out of the Brighton Beach apartment and into Bay Ridge, and he began to spend all his free time sitting in the coffeeshop and talking endlessly to anyone who would listen about the dangers of raising children in this hell of a place. In spite of his partiality to drink, he started to visit the Islamic Center regularly. He liked to sit and talk with the imam of the mosque and would sometimes even run little errands for him. He began to do volunteer work for the center; he specialized in making funeral arrangements for people from the community with the Muslim cemetery in New Jersey. He was the one who bought the white cloth for the shrouds, the incense, and anything else the family needed. Sometimes other volunteers would pile into his car and they would drive behind the hearse to the cemetery where prayers would call on God to raise the departed soul to His eternal Paradise and to forgive the body about to be buried in a non-Muslim land. Newly arrived refugees went to him for advice about where to go shopping or where to find housing or Arab cafés and restaurants and how to guard children from the corruption of their new home ("God have mercy on us all"). Abd al-Karim was also a firm believer in the Twin Towers conspiracy theory circulated in anonymous letters that instructed the receiver to copy and send on to the largest number of people possible ("so that God may multiply your good deeds"). The letter explained the miracle of the Quran and how it had predicted the events of September 11 and the destruction of the Cities of Injustice. Hend sits by herself opposite Abd al-Karim, who hands her a new piece of paper every time he sees her, a piece of paper that, as always, she has no desire to read.

She smokes her water pipe and gazes at the faces of the regular clients. When she senses that another argument is about to erupt, she decides to leave. She buys a pack of cigarettes and sits on a bench by the seaside watching the sun as it sinks into the vast Atlantic, then she takes the bus back home. Always, when nostalgia, loneliness, or self-loathing pulls her back to Bay Ridge, he categorically refuses to go with her:

"I don't want to go to that place."

"Why not?"

"It's dirty. And it's *vulgar*," he moans in English. "I don't want to be one of them."

"We can eat some Egyptian noodles."

"I don't want to!" he bawls hysterically.

"Are you going to make Mama go alone?"

"Why do you like it so much?"

"Maybe because it reminds me of home."

"But I don't like Bay Ridge! And I don't want to go back to Egypt either."

The Green Cemetery

Seventh Avenue runs through Greenwood Cemetery, which sits on a hill that reminds her of Pharaoh's Hills back home. She likes to wander its winding avenues early in the morning because of the flowers, and because of the profound silence that used to frighten her. She passes the time reading the names of the dead who lie beneath the marble slabs. The elation of death and oblivion, the peacefulness of old people washes over her. The houses that face the cemetery are also old, with stiff marble facades. Elderly Russian and Hispanic women sit in wooden rocking chairs on their porches. The Latino ladies carefully step out of gaily colored houses into the pale winter sunlight, houses that put the gray hues of other neighborhoods to shame. They smile at her like children. She smiles back and walks on with leaden, worried steps, as though she were approaching an ending of some kind. The sturdy coat that she bought at a thrift store smells of mothballs and mold. It weighs on her body, heavy and forlorn. She disappears inside it, seamlessly blending into her surroundings: the old women and the streets, cold, solitary, neutral.

She has become more like her grandmother than her mother, she thinks to herself. She remembered how she used to squirm in her grandmother's lap, an angry child with a naked bottom. She was hard to keep up with as a child, light and thin, teething and crawling and speaking well before any of her brothers did. She proved that she was a creature capable of surviving and flourishing on the barest necessities of life. Her mother often left her to her own devices. She would crawl up the hill behind the western balcony right up to the solitary room roofed in wood and clay that looked, for all the world, like a heavenly dome. They called it 'the high place.' A woman sat at its door, a woman whom they did not call 'grandmother' but rather 'the Guest,' though she never once stepped out of the confines of the family home. "The Guest is sleeping," they would say, or "The Guest wants such and such," or "Go bring the buttermilk pan from the Guest's room."

The Guest was a tiny, timid peasant woman with a green tattoo on her chin. The back of her hand was also covered with tattoos — a bride, a fish, and a lion. Her room always smelled of perfumed candles. She wove rope out of long strands of fiber and mended the holes in old clothes. Her dresses too were embroidered with tiny lions and fishes and dolls. Little Hend would crawl after her mother for half the day, crying and trying to catch hold of the hem of her long robe: "Mama sit. Mama *dees*" (Mama sit down so I can nurse). And because her mother was constantly running around taking care of the housework, she would always send her to the Guest's room. The Guest had no work to keep her busy. She would take the squirming Hend into her lap and stroke her back until she fell asleep. Or she would teach her how to stretch out her hand and feed the chicks and the baby ducklings with the leftovers from a carton box. When the Guest died, they prayed for her soul: "Her hand was blessed. . . . May God have mercy on her," adding, "if she bore witness to the One God before the Angel came to take her away."

Says her mother: "Your grandfather Muqawi was big and strong and bedded both slave and freewoman, Arab and non-Arab. But the peasant girl from the Coptic Estate — she was the only one who bore him children. May God rest her soul, if she truly testified before the Angel came for her."

And this was how Hend came to understand — after the Angel of Death had swept through their house — that the woman who had lived in that solitary room was her grandmother; a small peasant woman who came from the Coptic Estate or 'the White Estate' in the days before the Nur Mosque (as the people called it), with its enormous marvel of a marble dome, had been built. She was a young girl with the ragged cloth belt of impoverished agricultural day laborers tied around her waist. One day, the Chief of Bedouins with his regal headdress passed through the fields on his stallion and saw the delicate white flowers of the cotton plant blooming from that belt. He looked at the girl's belly, puffed up with cotton blossoms, and straightaway divined the auspicious signs of a fertile seed. "She will surely be the mother of a male child," he said to himself. "The Prophet himself—peace and blessings upon him—begat from a Coptic woman." Then he pulled her up by the arm onto his horse and rode off with her. The girl's father, bent and filthy, ran after them brandishing a lump of the fecund mud in his hands. "With God's blessings," he murmured, after the sheikh placed a coin of pure gold in his astonished palm.

She undid the dirty belt from her waist so that he could look upon the body that was like a piece of smooth white cheese. The body, rounded like a morsel of moist halva, surrendered to his touch. The grandmother—whose name would soon become 'the Guest'—bathed for the first time in a basin of pure copper and combed out the long, luxuriant hair that Hend would inherit. The fish tattoos flexed and gleamed in the water that streamed over her body and the servants sang to her from the other side of the door.

Whose daughter is this in the village,
you whose shawl has been caught?
I'm betrothed to the Chief of Arabs,
he whose uncle is a prince.

The Chief of Bedouins disliked houses because of their low, cramped roofs. He lived in a large tent pitched in the middle of an open expanse of land. His wives lived in the compound in a series of adjoining mud-brick rooms that opened onto the sandy court-yard. On the other side stood a similar row of rooms, the kitchens and granaries. A group of palm trees stood between the two rows. The Guest was not given one of these rooms in the main compound. She was like a frightened she-camel and it would take her some time to settle down. The grandfather built two rooms for her alone up on one of the smaller elevations of Pharaoh's Hills. She never visited the women down below and not once did she cross the perimeters of the main compound. She never witnessed the hustle and bustle of the kitchens nor smelled the pungent odors of milling day. She would hear the noise and guess at what was happening in the granaries. From a distance she would watch the shadows of the women running back and forth between the rooms. The Guest would sit in front of her house and wait for the young servant girls, pungent with kitchen odors, to come to her. They would step inside quickly and set her meal down with a perfunctory greeting, then run back outside without giving her a chance to exchange a single word. They never called her "Mistress" or "Auntie," only "the Guest" or "the master's foreign woman," names that were a summing up of her place in the world.

Her husband brought her precious gifts of Damascene silk and fine cotton cloth from Ashmun. Whenever loneliness crept over her, she would run her hand over one of her black velvet gowns and, taking up the needle, begin to embroider its bodice with sequins and little bits of colored glass. A rope on which she hung these gowns stretched along the length of the wall of her room. As time passed, the gowns piled up on the rope and it sagged like her breasts, from the burden of the heavy weight.

She would perfume her gowns with incense and musk and lay them out in the eye of the noonday sun—to preserve them from moth eggs, or perhaps to provoke the envy of her co-wives. At night she would stuff their pockets with henna and basil leaves and stow them away under the mattresses to smooth out the creases. Then she would sit and keep watch on the gates of the high encircling wall from the corner of her eye.

The Guest was not inclined to conversation. On the rare occasions when she did speak, she would tell the same story about the husband who owned a caravan of camels laden with wooden chests that traveled between Gaza and Khan Yunis. The chests were piled high with grain and they came back with olive oil and bars of Aleppo soap, robes of silk and Meccan velvet and Yemeni incense. The wives of this husband were many, she says, but it was she alone who mothered a male child.

The Guest says: "As soon as I emptied my belly of an infant, I'd put him in the basket and send him to the big tent for his father to hold. The child would come back silent and listless every time, and after a night or two, his face would puff up and turn blue and then he would die. When the fifth boy-child came, I said to myself, 'The evil eye can shatter rock.' I piled rags over the basket and said to the women, 'The boy has died. He's followed his brothers.' Then I placed him on my breast and he nursed, sleepy and soft like a ball of white cotton. Our Lady Mary came to me in my sleep and took him from my breast and plunged him in holy water and in the morning he was pink and white like a rose. The Savior and the Virgin decreed that he should live when I feared he would go to the place the others had gone. Then I sent him to his father and he said, 'God be praised' and named him Ibrahim."

The Guest loved to exercise her nimble fingers. She loved to willow cotton, peel garlic, and strip corncobs of their brittle husks. She twisted rope out of fiber and the wicks of kerosene lamps out of cotton and she wove mats out of strips of bamboo. If she had nothing else to weave, she would twist thin paper cones out of bits of old newspapers; these she used to light the kerosene lamps in order to save matches. On that hill opposite the tent of the Chief of Bedouins, she would weave and sing and see after her hens. From time to time she would dip her feet into the running waters of the canal. She was a peasant and could not live without soil and animals.

Little Hend would fall asleep in the Guest's lap as she flung open the gates to her world of marvelous stories. She always began these stories in the same way. "If our house were close by . . ." she would whisper, "if our house were close by . . . ." And yet she had no other house. Her house was their house. Hend would squat next to her as she emptied the cotton stuffing from the pillowcases onto the floor and spread it out in the sun, pulling it to make it light and fluffy like spun sugar. In the grandmother's stories, the maidens endlessly labor over the recalcitrant cotton, pulling and teasing it for the velvety smooth pillows that will receive the sweat of love and childbirth, and the tears of desertion and loss. The pillows that cradle our sleeping faces and catch our dreams at night should be soft and secret. Hend lays her head in the Guest's lap and listens to her tell a story: "If my father's house were close by . . . ."

"Where is your father's house?" the girl interrupts her. The Guest laughs as she tries to remember. "Near the village threshing ground? Past the Valley of the Angel? Behind the salt marshes on the White Estate?" (The grandmother does not know that the White Estate on which she lived is now called the Mosque Estate.) She says, trying to pinpoint the very moment: "One day, your grandfather, may he rest in peace, passed our way. I was standing there at the door of the house . . . sweeping the floor? No! I was picking cotton in the fields of the Bedouin tribes. . . ." She tells the story of how he came and took her away on his horse and shut her up in a house with high walls. The Guest gazes at the open sky but she can't tell east from west, and she does not know if any member of her family is still alive. She still dreams of walking along the bank of that faraway canal, of scrubbing her dress in the running water, and scraping the heels of her feet on a sieve at the top of a field planted with broad beans. She strings broad beans together in necklaces that Hend wears around her neck. Hend hops around her grandmother like a rabbit and scurries off to run her errands. The Guest sends her from time to time to buy a few candles from Salim the druggist's shop. When Hend returns, she plies her with questions about a long-ago world.

"Is Salim still alive?"

Hend nods her head.

"Does he still run the shop?"

Hend shakes her head.

"Who's at the counter?"

Hend moves her lips lazily to form a brief answer. "His son."

"Is Abu Ma'tuq's house still opposite Salim's shop?"

Hend doesn't know who Abu Ma'tuq is. She doesn't recognize half the names that the Guest remembers, but she nods her head to assure her that everything is still just as it is in her imagination. The threshing machine still stands on the edge of the Bedouin field opposite the Muqawi Aqueduct and the migrant laborers still live in the salt marshes. All those folk that peopled her memory—shop owners, carpenters, fishmongers—were still there, as she remembered them to be long ago.

Hend had no idea why they called her the Guest, nor why her clothes were stowed away in a wooden chest as though she were ever on the verge of embarking on some voyage or other, or why she took out her velvet gown at the beginning of each season, perfumed it, then carefully refolded it and placed it back in the wooden chest. Hend was mesmerized by the dark freckles stamped on her face, the same ones she has inherited along with the long hair, the short stature, and a dark and brooding disposition.

She herself is still that same restless child, she muses, always looking for a suitcase in which to pile clothes grown tired of being shut up in closets, a traveling case that she can place under her pillow for safekeeping, a thing to be seized and whisked away in anger, a thing to rest her head upon in sorrow. In her dreams she sees the Guest passing her fingers over her palm and stroking the life line there. She laughs and says, "The way of Abu Zayd the Wanderer." Hend did not know then that her life would become a smoldering fire, a long exile, like that of the legendary Abu Zayd. Her restless spirit was no longer content with stories of fleet camels and noble steeds and fiery comets shooting through the corridors of the sky. The journey of winter and summer in those stories was not enough to plug the pit of fear in her heart. Hend slept in the Guest's lap whenever she grew tired of the coarse, cruel pillows that refused to give up their tenderness. In the dream she says to her:

If my father's house were close by
I'd go and bring a plate of raisins
for you to eat and then you'd pray over the beloved
for all lovers pray to God to pray for the beloved.

Sleep overcomes her and the dreams that come carry her across the seven seas.

Then the dreams came true at a single stroke. Here she is now, walking down Flatbush Avenue without a map. She has come to know a good number of streets by heart. She spends her days sitting in front of the huge discount supermarket where she often shops. She examines the store circular and compares. She's learned the essential words by now, words like 'savings' and 'coupons' and 'buy one get one free.' She walks through Greenwood Cemetery and examines the crosses on the tombstones and tries to forget the grandmother who lived in a small house on top of the hill and never once left it.

The grandmother died hugging her wooden cross to her chest and was buried in the family crypt with the following epitaph: "The Guest, mother of children, God rest her soul and lead her into His vast gardens of Paradise." She left nothing behind but a small wooden chest in which she had packed her many dresses of satin and velvet embroidered with fishes and dolls, and a short rope on which had hung a gown of black velvet, fragrant and still, never once soiled by the dusty ground. In a smaller cardboard box she left a few candles and needles and bits of soap, while in the nooks and crannies of the room she had carefully placed a few stray strands of the hair that had fallen out over the years from pregnancy and childbirth, the death of suckling babes, and the endless days, both white and black.

Windsor Terrace

M r. Windsor used to live on Fourth Avenue before it became Fourth Avenue. Long ago, the entire area was made up of Dutch farms spreading out over the fertile slope of eastern Brooklyn. The Saturday market was the last remaining trace of that distant world. It was a vegetable and poultry market, mostly frequented by artists shopping for natural or 'organic' foods and enchanted by the din and the air of nostalgia that hovered about the place. Hend liked the Fourth Avenue market because the prices were reasonable and she could bargain there. She liked to sit on the sidewalk of the wide avenue on Saturdays and watch the young women in the stiff brown wigs that hid their shaved heads going in and out of the Jewish synagogues nearby.

She stared at their long black skirts and heavy coats curiously. They nodded their heads shyly at her and sometimes they stopped to ask if she was Jewish. She would quickly shake her head in the negative before they got a chance to hand her one of their flyers: printed invitations to visit the House of God. She preferred to steer clear of those kinds of invitations. The sidewalk of Fourth Avenue was wide like a terrace and it hosted a secondhand market that they call a *flea market* in English. Things no longer wanted by their owners are piled up on the pavement for sale: kitchen utensils, old clothes and shoes, wooden boxes, framed paintings, photo albums whose owners were long dead, records with pictures of

Elvis Presley, Liza Minnelli, or Frank Sinatra on the sleeve, antique cameras, entire libraries spilling out of their cartons, notebooks still carrying the imprint of their owners' fingers. The most intimate moments of ordinary people transformed into stacks of abandoned memories, legacies to be picked over by cheerful amateur collectors once the bones of their former owners had finally been deposited in Greenwood Cemetery. Hend liked to sit with Emilia as she spread out her wares on the pavement. She knew all the styles and brand names of her old shoes by heart, and she priced them according to decade of origin: 1950s, 1960s, and 1970s. "They call this stuff 'vintage,'" she told Hend. "I don't know why Americans are so crazy about it. Maybe it comes in handy for Halloween parties and such. All the young actor-types around town know me. They come all the way from Manhattan: 'Hey Emilia, I need a pair of Marilyn Monroe shoes.' Those crazy kids are always looking for outlandish things."

Hend passed through Windsor Terrace daily because her son's school was nearby. She liked the wide streets and the way the meager winter sun passed slowly across the sky above. She liked to watch the old women sitting out in the sun like her, and trying to recollect the years that had vanished so quickly. She liked to sit on the wooden bench and watch Jojo tell fortunes from across the street. Emilia sits next to her and smiles. Her gray coat looks exactly like the one Hend is wearing. She's short and thin, with a slight stoop. Her face is covered in fine wrinkles and tufts of white hair sprout from unexpected places, like her nostrils and the edges of her upper lip. Her eyes are sharp and alert. They look like two round balls of fire, and when she opens her mouth wide to laugh she exposes a row of stained, broken teeth. She pulls her coat up around her when she sits down and takes off her shoes and socks to sun her feet. She swings her bare, swollen legs back and forth as though she were a child on a swing, and the downy hair that covers them gleams in the sunlight. Emilia likes to talk a lot, and when she gets started on the story of her long life it's almost impossible to interrupt her. She keeps mysterious coupons in a cloth purse and organizes them carefully so that she can find exactly what she wants when she needs it. She talks with great authority about how to save pennies and where to find the cheapest stuff but she also loves to philosophize about life.

Hend met her for the first time at the library, at a talk about how the media shapes public opinion in the United States. Emilia was sitting in the front row because she was hard of hearing, as Hend later found out. She had simply removed the "reserved" sign on the chair and sat down. Hend was sitting right behind her and, before the event had even gotten under way, Emilia started talking to anyone who would listen about the meaning of critical thinking. She said that she was a citizen of the former Soviet Union and that she had emigrated to America with her husband in the 1970s during the Cold War. Her husband—who had retired long ago—used to be a physics professor and he had come to the States as a political refugee. She talked about how she had lived her whole life in a country with an official state media, but that after twenty years of living in New York (she was now almost eighty years old) she had grown even more tired of the supposedly 'free' media here. It reminded her of the old Soviet days, the propaganda, the calculated manipulation of people's tastes, thoughts, and choices. Now the only thing she watched was Dr. Phil, and sometimes Oprah, while her husband preferred to watch the BBC. She had come to America without knowing a single word of English. She and her husband had moved into a mixed Russian and Latino neighborhood, and she could have easily spent the rest of her life without learning any English at all. But she liked to listen to the tiny transistor radio that she took everywhere with her and that's how she learned to speak the language.

Emilia talked on and on without pausing once. The panelists looked at each other in dismay and wondered who was going to be the one to gently put an end to her homily on American television and radio. No one dared. She was a forceful speaker, and always

41

on high alert against any attempt to shut her down. People in the audience began to drift off, one after the other, some quietly, others muttering angrily, until no one was left except for Hend, who remained sitting right behind her, waiting. That was the beginning of their friendship. Emilia's easy, undemanding companionship was soothing to Hend, and Emilia grew attached to Hend because she listened to her quietly till the very end, and went along with her to book discussions and lectures. Emilia always came up with clippings and fliers advertising upcoming events of that kind, and she meticulously noted dates and times and venues in a little notebook that she kept for the purpose. She often called Hend to invite her to this or that event. The two women enjoyed being alone in each other's company.

Emilia's husband hated going out. He liked to cook and do the housework as he listened to his favorite classical music. He worshiped peace and quiet and so he never gave Emilia the chance to open her mouth. Emilia would wait for Hend every morning on the wooden bench in front of the green market on Fourth Avenue. Together they soaked in the thin sunlight and drank coffee out of paper cups. They watched the passersby and exchanged food coupons and news about free events or classes: dancing and cooking classes; street fairs and cultural festivals: the Middle Eastern Festival, the Brooklyn Jazz Festival; book signings at the library, and so on.

They sit together in silence, like carbon copies perched on a paradoxical wooden bench. They gaze out at the emptiness of the park and into the last rays of the stingy winter sun. Emilia begins to lay out the coupons that she doesn't really need. She gives Hend the ones for diapers and baby food. Then, as though suddenly remembering something, she asks her: "How old is your son?"

"Eight," Hend replies.

Emilia takes the coupons back from Hend and puts them in her purse. "Okay. Take this instead." But Hend refuses.

"You're still young, you can use this stuff."

Hend shakes her head again. "I don't need them any more."

"You're still young. It's only temporary."

"It stopped years ago."

Emilia nods her head sympathetically. "I got menopause when I came to this country. I was still young back then . . . 57 years old."

Hend just nods her head and doesn't say anything. Emilia gets up all of a sudden and crosses the street over to her Mexican friend Jojo's storefront. Jojo is Abd al-Karim's ex-wife, and she tells fortunes now. A sign hangs in the glass window: *Your fortune told. Palm readings, zodiac, tarot.*

Hend sits there on the bench by herself, clutching coupons for sanitary napkins that she doesn't need. Her eyes fall on the spider web of thin varicose veins that has sprouted on her leg. She slowly tears up the coupons into small pieces and throws them into the empty coffee cup.

Emilia comes and goes, for no particular reason, without hellos or goodbyes. Now she comes back and sits next to her again, picking up the threads of a conversation that she alone can begin and end. She smells like all old people: an obscure, indecipherable smell that time deposits without making any excuses. Hend knows that smell well from her childhood days, when she used to trail around after an old woman who worked in her father's house. People used to call her Grandmother Zaynab from before anyone could remember. Grandmother Zaynab was chocolate brown but when she stood in front of the clay oven in the courtyard her skin took on the color of dry crusty bread. She would spill a pail of washing water over her bare neck and chest, which were burning hot from the stinging flames of the oven, then wet an old rag in the pail to wipe down the oven rack. A small woman squatted behind her to help her with the baking. As soon as Grandmother Zaynab eased a loaf into the mouth of the oven, she would say, "Hand me another one, sister," and the woman would scoop out a round lump of dough in the palm of her hand and place it on the bread paddle. The balls of dough were magically transformed into perfectly formed loaves of bread as they came out of the oven's mouth.

Grandmother Zaynab was not her grandmother. She was no relative at all. Her voice rang with that Delta accent that distinguished the outsiders from the Bedouin. Her official job was to bake the family's weekly bread but she would also come to prepare for the dough-making ritual. She washed the wheat and spread it out on bamboo mats, scented it with grains of fenugreek and lupine and rough corn, and carried it on her head to the distant mill. She kept the keys to the grain storerooms, scrubbed the kneading basins, and collected the dry tree leaves to fuel the oven. Every Friday she came to sprinkle the corners of the house with blessed herbs and water and salt, murmuring invocations against the evil eye of the enviers: *There is no might or grace save in God.* She gave the people of the house enchanted water to drink to chase away mischievous spirits and prepared steaming earthenware pots of pigeons and rice on feast days like Ashura and Ragabiya and the first of Sha'ban. People said that her hand was blessed. She would dip it in olive oil and rub the mother's constantly aching back, or set the bones of the boys who were always tripping and falling and breaking their legs from bouncing off the walls. Grandmother Zaynab was not their servant. There was nothing about her that suggested this. She worked in other houses besides theirs, delivering babies and tying the umbilical cords of newborns, treating aches and pains with ointments made from camphor and linseed oil and plaster with an agile and practiced hand. Her forehead boasted a green tattoo in the form of a fish. Another plastic fish hung from a cord around her neck and the same green fishes also decorated her wrist. Her nostrils were split from the weight of a ring that had once ornamented her nose and left behind a sharp vertical slash.

Grandmother Zaynab's hair was like white cotton candy. She used to rub the part of her hair with soft butter to make it shine. She moved through the house like a length of thin, dry, hollowed-out sugarcane, a heavy anklet of pure silver clasped around her skinny leg. She lived in a mud hut that had been built against the wall of the baking rooms. Hend used to climb the low wall straight into the heart of Grandmother Zaynab's house. "Grandmother, Mama wants you." A little while later, Grandmother Zaynab would come to the house to milk the cows and make the cheese and collect the eggs and check up on the duck sitting on her chicks. She packed the coals into the water pipe and the thick smoke crept out of her split nose as she laughed. "The pipe chases away the ghouls in your head."

Grandmother Zaynab regularly attended Sheikha Safina's weekly exorcism. She put on her green gown on Thursday market day and wrapped her head in a white scarf. She came back from the market and laid her bundles down on the ground. "I'm going to the dakka," she would curtly inform them. "I'll see you later." She disappeared from high noon to sunset and always came back exhausted and speechless. She would lay her body down in the western balcony and passersby would hear her talking to her qarina sleepily.

When Hend went into the baking room that day, all she wanted was to watch the soft, hot bread coming out of the burning mouth of the oven. "Give me a little one, Grandmother," she murmured, mesmerized by the movement of the bread paddle sliding the soft dough into the oven. A 'little one' was a miniature loaf of bread made especially for children. Grandmother Zaynab, who was busy finishing her story, ignored the girl. ". . . And I said, by God, don't you dare raise your hand against me!" Hend knew that Grandmother Zaynab was telling the story of her first husband to her qarina. She had heard the story many times before: "He started hitting me on my face and saying, 'Where were you, you bitch?' and me saying to him, 'I had to fulfill my vow to Sheikha Safina.' He didn't let go of me until he had knocked out this big tooth," and she opens her mouth to show her qarina the big gap there. Hend repeats herself irritably, "I want a little one *now*, Grandmother." But the Grandmother was busy talking and wiping down the top of the oven. "He left me lying there just like this old rag, sister." She points to the ash rag, then adds, "He went to do his ablutions at the canal bridge and he started invoking the Prophet's name, but he'd forgotten that the switchblade he'd just slashed me with was still in his pocket. It was sharp!" and she points to a jagged scar on her face. "I warned him, 'God's command! God's prohibition!' But he had no faith in God or man. The switchblade cut into his stomach as he was washing himself for prayer and he was already done for by the time they brought him home to me."

Hend was bored of listening by now, and angry at Grandmother Zaynab for ignoring her. "Come on, Grandmother!" she shouted impatiently.

The Grandmother's face grew red like a burning coal and she picked up a piece of firewood and waved it furiously at her. "Get out of here, girl! No little ones for you."

They were used to her sudden inexplicable fits of anger. She would shoo away the children like a barren bitch, then a few minutes later turn around and pat their heads with her rough hand, dip the 'little one' in molasses, and feed the open mouths around her in a gentle token of peace. Hend wasn't afraid of her, though. She scooped up a handful of dirt from the ground and threw it in her face. The second time she did it, the dirt settled on the soft balls of dough. She ran off and didn't stop running until she got to the flame tree and scurried up it breathlessly. Grandmother Zaynab ran after her, brandishing a long stout stick and shouting threats. When Hend finally came down, the rough hand seized her, dragged her into the dark room, and shut the old wooden door fast. Half the day went by with her locked up behind that door. The damp mud room was full of hidden rabbit lairs and piles of green clover. The rabbits hopped around surreptitiously in the clover, suddenly emerging into the open with twitching jaws, then scurrying back, trembling, into their holes. Hend sat there on the black basalt stone behind the door and stared at the dark holes as the skylights above sifted the meager light coming in from the washed-out crimson sky.

Grandmother Zaynab eventually came back carrying the miniature loaf of bread and some honey but the girl, who had wet herself, didn't open her mouth. She made her drink some enchanted water from the fright pan, and then she made her jump seven times over a bowl of burning Javanese incense, but it didn't do any good. Hend grew listless and her eyes took on a strange, faraway look. A few days later she claimed that she had seen Grandmother Zaynab in the shape of a green toad the color of clover hopping around on the pile of vegetable scraps, and that she had stuck out her white lizard tongue at Hend and ordered her to lick her belly and then swallow the saliva afterward. Hend was afraid of the dark and of the scurrying rabbits, so she did it. She licked the green toad's belly and then she wet herself. She kept on wetting herself for many years after that and the pungent, acrid smell of urine clung to her clothes no matter what she did.

Grandmother Zaynab stayed at their house for weeks after this incident. She sprinkled blessed herbs throughout the house and chanted magical incantations. She washed the girl's body in rose-water and dressed her in a spotless white dress and took her to see Sheikha Safina. She lit seven candles in the Sheikha's window and said, "By your darling Prophet, don't fail me now. I'm the one who scared the wits out of the girl." But Hend kept wetting herself. In her dreams, the green toad pursued her down secret subterranean passages, foamy spittle leaking from its mouth.

Grandmother Zaynab ruffles Hend's hair and yawns, then she starts to tell her stories about long-ago travelers. Her sharp eyes pick out a few gray hairs that have begun to sprout on the girl's head—a girl who is not yet ten—and she notices that the roots have begun to turn white too. So she puts the henna to soak in boiled tea with black seed, then applies it to Hend's long hair, transforming it into a curtain of deep black and flaming red. The white embers cleave the roots and sprout again. Grandmother Zaynab sighs in despair and says, "I don't know what to do with this daughter of yours, mistress." Her mother adds three new nicknames for Hend to her list: "the little demon," "loopy," and "head-in-the-clouds."

Here she is now, walking as always next to Emilia in a place called Brooklyn. They stroll up and down the wide sidewalks of Fourth Avenue so that Emilia can inspect cartons full of bric-a-brac that their owners have thrown away: books and pictures, anything that has gotten old and useless and disposable. Hend reads the phrase *take me if you want* printed in magic marker on the sides of the cartons. She wonders at this oblique expression, and she feels that it is somehow directed at her.

Emilia rummages around in the cartons for old shoes and empty bottles. She pokes around slowly and patiently in garbage cans. On Saturdays, she takes her choicest treasures to the corner of Windsor Terrace and spreads them out next to the other vendors. Emilia specializes in shoes. "Marilyn Monroe shoes," she calls out to passersby. "I've got Audrey Hepburn, Farrah Fawcett. . . . I've got kids' shoes too."

Hend tells her that she reminds her of so many people she's met in her life. Emilia laughs, revealing the gaps in her mouth where teeth used to be. "I know, I know. Everybody says that I look like the old woman in *Zorba the Greek*. It's too bad I never saw that movie. I don't know about Mrs. Zorba, but all old people look alike, my dear."

Scattered raindrops fall on Emilia's frail, wrinkled face. Hend leaves her to her never-ending task of poking through abandoned cardboard boxes. She goes to sit on the wooden bench in front of her son's school while her eyes follow Emilia as she moves farther and farther away, pushing the little cart piled high with shoes that fit and others that don't.

Coco Bar

The smell of fresh beer wafts up from old wooden barrels in the little bar right under her window. She likes the smell of beer because it reminds her of her father. Grandmother Zaynab used to say, "Your father was popular with the ladies, God rest his soul. He used to walk around the Heights and the girls would sing to him from behind their windows. Fatma al-Qarumiya used to compose poetry about him:

He's the lovely one who passed beneath our window
beneath our window his lips drip honey
beneath our window, and what can I do, girls?
beneath our window, he's the lovely one who passed through.

He was handsome and refined, and he always wore elegant suits. That's what Hend still remembers about her father. It was a lot of extra work for her mother. She ironed his white pocket handkerchiefs, folded and organized his socks, and carefully matched his neckties. Another photo in the family album: her father stands in front of the auditorium of the Faculty of Law at King Fouad University, looking trim and smart. For some reason that Hend doesn't fully understand, he never took a job after graduation. He hung a sign that said "Lawyer for Misdemeanors in the Civil Courts" on the door of the reception house on the hill, but he didn't have an office or clients, and he never attended court proceedings except when he wanted to see his friends. Every day he left the house in his elegant suit, his vest unbuttoned, his black hair slicked back with Vaseline, and strolled down the alleys where he was known as a distinguished man of leisure. He passionately attended all the agricultural cooperative meetings, the municipal assembly meetings, and the local council meetings. All of these organizations occupied the same red-brick building in the center of the town and her father's educated friends were all to be found there: Doctor Shamil the pharmacist, Mr. Emile the school principal, and His Excellency the President of the Municipal Assembly, whoever he happened to be at the time.

These were the same men who would regularly meet in the evenings in her father's cozy reception house. It was a small house perched high above Pharaoh's Hills where a woman called 'the Guest' used to live. Hend would constantly find excuses to go there. She would climb up the hill bringing him anything he might need: "Father do you want dinner, Father do you want fresh clothes, Father do you want some snacks?" Her mother prepared small trays of homemade pickles and boiled broad beans marinated in lemon juice and Hend carried them up to the reception house. Sometimes her mother sent her to ask for money. Hend hated carrying that particular message. Her brothers simply refused to do it. The daily negotiation over money was always conducted through her. Sometimes her father would explode into a barrage of curses that she knew by heart: "Money, money, money! Do you think I'm sitting on a money machine? Minting shitty new coins every day?" But faced with Hend's unflinching, reproachful gaze, he would finally give in and hand her a few silver coins from his pocket. Sometimes, Hend would go back empty-handed with the following curt message: "I don't have any." Her mother's nose would color slightly, then she would sigh heavily after listening to Hend repeat those four words that seemed to encapsulate the entire story of her misfortunes, and Hend knew that this sigh was the harbinger of a breakdown that was sure to envelop the whole house in a flood of misery and gloom.

Sometimes she went up to the reception house for no particular reason. "Mama says go see if your father wants anything," was the innocent phrase she used as a password. Only she was allowed to play this little trick. Her father always had a smile for his little girl. He could never manage to be harsh with her, even if he tried.

After the death of the Guest, her father hung his sign on the door to remind everyone that he was still officially a lawyer at the Higher Court of Appeals. In point of fact he believed that the courts were a waste of time, and that reception houses like his were the proper place to solve disputes. He spent every evening up there with his friends. Hend would sometimes hear Fatma al-Qarumiya's voice coming from inside and the ring of her long voluptuous laugh mingling with the laughter of the men, but on those occasions she never dared to disturb them.

At school, everyone respected Hend because her father always made a point of attending the parents' meetings that no one ever went to. The first time he went, he sat with the school principal, Mr. Emile, and they chatted about things like the importance of raising the town's abysmal educational standards. Her father offered Mr. Emile one of his red Dunhill cigarettes and the man practically fainted with joy as he accepted the proffered cigarette and launched into his favorite subject. "Your Excellency, I've got more than one hundred students in my school and the municipality doesn't give us a single penny, not even to fix the school bell. Imagine, your Excellency, I have to use this whistle to signal the start of classes!" Her father knew that Emile spent most of his spare time sitting in front of the small bicycle repair shop (which also doubled as a warehouse) that he had recently opened next to the school courtyard, but he quickly became a bosom friend of her father's. Hend would watch him busily preparing plates of hot sausage in the reception house and setting out cold bottles of beer as he laughed out loud at some joke or other. The sound struck Hend as strange, because Mr. Emile rarely laughed. From time to time he would declare, "By God, your Excellency, you've made our stay in this godforsaken place easier to bear. The village would have been terribly lonely without these little soirées of yours."

Hend knows that her father made life a lot more pleasant for the outsiders like Emile and Shamil, as well as the women who came to the village from other parts of the country. The reception house became a temporary home for some of them: Miss Ibtisam for example, the music teacher from Port Said who wore provocatively short skirts, and Miss Fayqa, the home economics teacher who taught her mother how to crochet the duck stitch. The reception house up on the hill hosted many a lady teacher for a few weeks at a time. Hend would take them their breakfast tray in the morning and their dinner tray in the evening, and at the end of their appointed stay some of them would come down to the house to thank her mother for her hospitality. They would sit with her for a little while in the western balcony and teach her how to crochet a new stitch or how to use hair curlers and dress a chignon. Some of them didn't come at all, though. Some contrived to make husbands of the village's petty bureaucrats while others left town pretty quickly because Pharaoh's Hills "is a tiny, bone-dry, backward village," or so they said. The nurses who worked at the local hospital were also habitués of the reception house and these women almost never went down to the main house to greet her mother. It was Doctor Shamil who introduced the new girls to their evening soirées and he ended up marrying more than one of them. Most of them simply disappeared as suddenly as they had appeared, leaving Fatma al-Qarumiya to laugh out loud in her opaque, masculine voice—the undisputed queen of the circle of men.

Her father's generosity was not limited to hosting itinerant female guests. He also liked to resolve hanging disputes between the local families. His powers of persuasion were superlative, what with his aristocratic looks, his clean, elegant suits, and his deep, melodious voice. Besides, the courts' tentacles were long and complicated and people preferred to avoid them if they could. The preparations for these reconciliation sessions were elaborate.

Clean rush mats were spread out on the floor of the reception house, pots of tea and coffee were served, and sometimes, if a satisfactory settlement was reached among the parties, small animals were slaughtered and roasted over an open fire. Her father, dressed in his beautiful Bedouin cloak, would lean back comfortably on the mat against a pile of pillows and reel off the relevant provisions of the criminal code, the sayings of the Imam Ali, and the counsel of the prophets, and back up his claims with ringing Quranic verses. The feuding clans were almost invariably persuaded to accept judgment of a few kilos of grain, five Egyptian pounds, or occasionally an inch of land separating their respective waterwheels, because "possession belongs to God alone." After the warm welcome, the tea and coffee and the elaborate feasting, the feuding parties would leave the reception house content and for the next few weeks, her father would be easy and cheerful.

Her mother puts on her honey-colored robe and says to him in a disapproving tone that he pretends not to understand: "Why do you always have to wear yourself out for other people?" He shakes his head wearily and replies, "You're the daughter of Bedouin Arabs. You of all people should understand our customs. You know it's a duty." When he calls her "cousin," her mother smiles one of her rare smiles because it means that he's pleased with her; that he'll sleep in his own bed for the next few days and that he'll narrate the story of the feud to her over and over and in great detail, carefully explaining exactly how he artfully managed to put an end to the crisis. However, if she crosses the red line, if she complains or criticizes too much, if she dares to say (in that angry, resentful voice of hers that he knows so well), "What have we got to do with all these problems? Banquets and parties and expenses every other day! My children come first and your own household is more important," the peaceful conversation will turn into a violent argument. He'll storm out angrily through the eastern door, shouting bitter remarks about grief and worry and tiresome women. He'll slam the glass door a couple of times and go spend the night in the reception house high above Pharaoh's Hills. He'll light the brazier and the air will become thick with the smell of incense and hashish and cigarette smoke and melancholy—not to mention Fatma al-Qarumiya's heavy perfume. Her deep laugh sets her plump white flesh shaking merrily: "I've told you time and again, cousin, living with women is a miserable state of affairs."

Her father liked to read. He read a lot because he wanted to seem like an expert on everything. He read biographies of Christopher Columbus and Edward Lane. He read about places he'd never seen before, like the lands of the White Nile and Mount Lebanon. He talked about Paris and Naples and Tangiers and he gave his friends in the reception house the impression that he was a seasoned traveler. They acted like they believed him because he spoke confidently and always came up with convincing details. Hend believed him too. She rode the sea of his imagination and saw ships and distant harbors there. His friends pretended to believe him for the sake of the party and the sheer delight of make-believe. Doctor Shamil told them all stories about how he had traveled to important conferences and invented new drugs for epilepsy and bed ulcers and arthritis. He was an expert at mixing up a special hashish and opium paste that he claimed could vanquish every disease but prostate cancer, for which, God preserve us, there was no cure. They would all laugh because they knew that the important conferences he went to were just a few dozen kilometers away in Alexandria, and that they were more often than not nothing but fishing expeditions for fair-skinned prostitutes. They also knew that he was badly addicted to the opium that whittled away at his brain. Emile liked to tell extravagant stories about his virility. He was short, thin, dark-skinned, and very hairy. The macho fantasies that he wove around his scrawny body were truly comic but everyone got a kick out of his risqué jokes because they went well with the sausages and cucumbers and pickles. Fatma al-Qarumiya meanwhile claimed that her ancestry went back to the Prophet's illustrious line in Mecca and that she was purer even than the folk heroine al-Khadra al-Sharifa. She was both a mother and a whore and the womanly smoke she blew out from her water pipe stirred up the men's admiration and provoked their lust.

He's been sleeping in the reception house for days now. Smoke drifts out from behind the door. Hend says, "Mama told me to come and ask if you want anything." They walk side by side, hands clasped. They pass the threshing machine and the Muqawi Aqueduct and a string of small mud houses. He points to things as they walk by. "That was your Grandfather Sulayman's estate, and this was your late Grandmother Shaqawa's guesthouse, and this is the Raml Aqueduct." She stumbles on the stones scattered in the sand as she walks next to him. On the way back home, tired and worn out, he smiles sadly. He gets into bed or stretches out in the balcony, and the children form a circle around him.

Her father was in the habit of drinking a beer or two before he went to bed every night. She would run over to Amm Mahmud's shop and say, "Two bottles of Stella beer and a pack of Dunhill cigarettes, please." He would stretch out on the rush mat in the eastern balcony and they clustered around him in a circle as he began to tell the story of the Prophet Moses. "Pray for the Prophet," he would say between each part of the story, but Hend preferred the story of the Prophet Joseph. She liked the sound of her father's sad voice as he told it in between mouthfuls of yellow foamy beer. "*Son, tell not thy vision to thy brothers lest they lay a trap for thee, for Satan is a mortal enemy of man.*" He liked to repeat that particular verse. He knew the Quranic text by heart and never made a mistake in pronunciation or punctuation. He slowly sipped at his beer as he talked. "He said, my son, enter not from the same door, rather enter from different doors." Her mother would sometimes interrupt the story to point out the dangers of the envier's evil eye. His head would be in her lap at this point, and her fingers would be playing with his hair while the children sat around his feet, small, wide-eyed, and hanging onto every word formed by that deep voice that drew them all like a magnet. As she listened, Hend dreamed of becoming a great prophet or saint, carrying a large rod with which to cleave the sea or running through the desert, plumes of water spurting up from beneath her feet. She was always fantasizing about being a character in an epic story, and her Arabic teacher encouraged these fantasies: "You'll do great things one day, God willing."

She began to seek out a real-world instrument for her greatness to manifest itself and found it in Angele, an easy victim. Angele was round and plump like a short, dark bear and she always sat at the back of the classroom, quiet and timid. Her features seemed to have been molded from a mixture of mud and sweat and they were stamped with an expression of astonishing simplicity. Hend began her self-appointed mission of guiding humanity with Angele. She would take her aside and talk to her about how she absolutely had to repeat the phrase "There is no god but God" so that she could enter the gates of Paradise as a good Muslim. Angele would shake her head miserably but Hend kept insisting. "Just say it in your head—the important thing is to go to Paradise." Angele took out a piece of soft bread filled with halva from her dirty cloth bag and held out half of it to Hend. "Want a piece of my sandwich?" That was how she always tried to change the subject and safely evade the iron grip of her would-be savior.

Angele was always lurking next to walls because she was afraid of running around and bumping into people. Her step was hesitant and slow; she was always kind to others but sometimes she acted terribly stupid. She didn't understand the jibes the other girls flung at her. She was resigned to it all—she was incapable of being any other way—and this dull indifference saved her a lot of trouble. She listened to all Hend's attempts to convert her without comment or resentment. She would just nod her head gently and say, "Only God can show us the way." She repeated this phrase as though it were a cheerful incantation; as though she truly believed that there might be some hope in this promised awakening to God's will after all. But Hend didn't give up on her chosen disciple until she disappeared from school altogether one day. Only then did she accept that she had definitively lost her first great battle in the war to deliver humanity from error.

Hend was the first girl at school to put on the long, flowing hijab. This was also part of her mission to transform herself into a story-book heroine. The other girls—even the peasant girls—wore light scarves on their heads that left their long, thick braids uncovered. Hend wrapped a thick, heavy scarf over her entire head. "God commanded women to wear the khimar, not a transparent scrap of cloth," she would proclaim in order to show off her piety and ascet-icism. She began to turn her eyes away from the sight of her father's evening bottle of beer and she often begged God to forgive him. Soon, many of the other girls followed her example and started wearing the heavy khimar to show that they were just as pious and modest. Not to be outdone in the fear of God, Hend went one step further and started wearing dark, forbidding colors: black or navy blue. She even took to wearing a pair of black gloves in public. ("I don't shake hands with men—may God curse those who do.") She trod a long road of self-abnegation and self-praise and she clung to it tenaciously, even after she had read the Quranic commentaries and discovered that the prohibition in question actually referred to bodies coming together in the act of love, and that it had noth-ing to do with a simple handshake. Nonetheless, she continued to insist that men and women were prohibited from shaking hands in Islam and that the act opened the door to lustful thoughts and actions. "Though hearts may meet in greeting, bodies will sink into sin," was a phrase she often repeated. She was one of the first girls at school to substitute the Islamic expression "God's peace upon you," an unusual greeting at the time, for the simple "Good morn-ing." She believed that all those who refused to pronounce God's peace in greeting sullied their hearts. She was constantly preoccu-pied with sin, constantly reading about it, parsing and interpreting it and hunting for the definitive bibliography of commentaries that would make her alone the possessor of its true meaning. She started a preaching meeting at school with a few fellow classmates.

She had a genius for making the other girls cry and feel the heavy burden of their guilt—any guilt. It made her spirits soar to see them in tears because her own long road began and ended in tears. While the other girls were busy with the school radio station and the wall newspapers and all the other extracurricular activities, she lowered her eyes and stifled her desires and went on acting the part of a great heroine, an instrument of God. For a long time, she really believed herself to be just that.

But in the same way that she had been the first girl to put on that long black curtain, she was the first one to discard it. Now she began to claim that modesty and beauty could comfortably coexist in God's eyes. She entered into a long, confusing period during which she dug around once again for the commentaries and legal opinions that would support her about-face with textual evidence that she could interpret as she liked. She was still busy being different. She exchanged the loose robes that she used to drag behind her in the dust for others that were shorter, tighter, and more flattering to the curves of her body: bright, colorful dresses whose sinfulness had yet to be proven beyond a shadow of a doubt. She unleashed a strategic strand of hair from beneath her head scarf, because God is merciful and compassionate and He would surely not consider her strand of hair to be a mortal sin. Here she is now, walking down Flatbush Avenue completely bare-headed, and no one is so much as glancing at her. But her eyes are still lowered out of habit. Her timid glances are the product of years of fear and frustration. She still wears loose clothes because her body is less than perfect, the flaccid body of a middle-aged woman whose hair is caught up in a severe bun just because she can't find the time to do it properly. She has to run around all day after the bus, to the market, to her son's school. The Latina women walking down the same street are dressed in tight skirts and pretty, revealing tops or short-shorts and no one bothers to look at them. They stretch out on the green grass of Prospect Park and their naked thighs lie open to the sun.

Hend crosses the park on her way to the library every day. She sits on the wide stone steps waiting for class to begin. Said sits next to her, smiling sweetly. She inspects the sweetness in his eyes and isn't sure how to interpret it. She looks at the vertical scar on his cheek and the tattoo on his chin, and she remembers that her father had a similar scar in the same place because he grew up at a time when bloodletting was the only treatment for any number of ailments. She doesn't understand why he has a tattoo, though: tattoos are for women, but it makes Said's smile seem broader and more inviting. Said always wears dark suits because he's a limousine driver. Sometimes he shares his halva or falafel sandwiches with her before class or after. These impromptu snacks are often interrupted by sudden telephone calls. He answers politely: "Yes, Father. Okay, Father." Afterward he explains to her that his parish priest wants him to do some volunteer work at the church. Said never told her how he ended up in America. He would only talk about his many relatives, the lottery, and the church's charitable work, and one day he shyly invited her on an outing, "Why don't you come and spend a Sunday with us and then we can go for a walk afterward?" She accepted because she liked his boyish, comical manner, and because he seemed to really enjoy her company. It was something she needed: someone to care for her, someone she might possibly love and be loved by; something to hold onto when everything else crumbled away. Hend often glimpsed the ghostly features of her only true friend in Said's face. This friend was born in the House of Capricorn. He had loved her sincerely and he died simply. She liked being with Said because he was kind and said sweet things to her. He reminded her of all the people she had cared for in her life.

The only church that Hend ever knew as a child was an unfinished structure that stood between the Hill Estate and Pharaoh's Hills. On her way to the schoolroom built by Mr. Wadie on top of the hill she always passed a few scattered houses. Mr. Wadie was the French teacher and he was married to Miss Ellen, the chemistry teacher, who had a small cross tattooed between her eyebrows. More and more teachers from the outside world came to Pharaoh's Hills. They always settled in and around the far-flung and inexpensive area near the schools. Mr. Wadie's house was next door to Mr. Emile the pharmacist's house and also to the houses of Mr. Mina, the Greek jeweler, and Madame Teresa, the seamstress. More teachers came to Pharaoh's Hills at the beginning of every school year: Mr. Samir Girgis, the math teacher, was one of them. Their houses huddled together in an intimate circle. The schoolroom sat on top of the hill, solitary and white. It was built of mud and plaster and it was bare but for a few chairs. Sometimes it smelled of burnt candles. Outside there were a few trees and a large metal sign: "Permit to build the Mother of Light Church on the Muqawi Estate, district capital of Pharaoh's Hills." Nearby, the Nur Mosque—also known as the Kuwaiti Mosque—would soon be born. It was named after the Kuwaiti sheikh who donated the funds for its construction. The mosque stood high and proud, with a tall minaret and marble steps and green carpets and taps that spouted cold water in summer. The town had never seen anything so luxurious before, but the small hill had trouble accommodating two buildings consecrated to God in such a tight space. The Mother of Light Church was consumed by fire every few months and rebuilt every time. After each fire, fights would break out. Mr. Wadie and some of his neighbors always took part in these brawls. The road to Mr. Wadie's house bristled with security details and was littered with broken pieces of colored glass from the windows of both buildings. New paths sprouted up on the hill and Hend began to avoid the area altogether. She still doesn't know if the Mother of Light Church was ever finished.

These are the memories of Pharaoh's Hills that have stayed with her. Everything else she's forgotten, because she now forgets a lot of things. She often leaves the food to burn on the stove and the smoke alarm disturbs her neighbors. She doesn't quite understand how she's stumbled into old age so suddenly and without warning.

Said picks her up in his limousine. He sits next to her in the big church with the high ceiling and she listens politely. The priest stands in front of her, neat and smiling in a simple gray suit, and welcomes her warmly, as does everyone else. They shake her hand energetically and introduce themselves without any fuss. They make her feel that she has always been one of them. She smiles politely and stands up when they do and sits down when they do. She nods her head at them and returns their smiles in kind. She listens closely to the sermon.

One day a man approached Christ to ask about his future. "You will die on your fortieth birthday, when your oldest son reaches the age of twenty-five," the Lord replied. The man, who did not have a son, wept, for he didn't want to die. Fearing the prophecy, he avoided marriage altogether and lived alone, never going near any woman. One day, a young man knocked on his door and begged leave to spend the night, as he was a traveler. In the morning, the young man shook his sleeping host and found him dead. Twenty years later, the young man discovered that the kind host who had taken him in and died on the morrow was his father.

Hend has heard different versions of this story, but she can't remember where or when. She muses on its significance. It seems to be saying that man is a pitiful creature. As far as Hend is concerned, there was no need for Christ or any other prophet to prove this truth. She nods her head wisely. The parable had moved her and she wants the others to see this. The man in the gray suit descends from the pulpit and shakes her hand again enthusiastically. He sits next to her and another priest takes his place in the pulpit. He too wears a gray suit and a wide smile, and he welcomes her publicly to the church. The congregation all turn to stare at her and smile. She is getting tired of all these smiles and nodding heads and decides to change the expression on her face to one of mute indifference. The second priest says, "A traveler met a wise man and asked him for counsel. The wise man pointed to his heart and said, 'Cultivate therein three things: modesty and the knowledge of sin, fear, and lastly courage, for if a heart understands not sin it will never change, and if it feels no fear it will discover no need to change, and if it possesses not courage it will be incapable of changing.'" Hend used to believe that she had managed to exorcize the ghost of sin that had accompanied her throughout her childhood and youth, and that she had finally freed herself of her fear, but she realized long ago that this was a lie. As she is making up her mind to leave, the hymns begin, rising from the lips of the congregation in powerful waves of sound.

In the corridors leading to the room where lunch has been laid out, she examines the pictures of Christian missions in familiar places: the alleys of Sohag, the neighborhoods of Darfur. A feeling of listlessness and despair creeps over her. It appeared that the only man who had asked her out in New York was trying to convert her. She feels nothing looking at the images of children who resemble her own son crowding around the milk cartons and relief supplies. She feels that she is nothing but an indefinite noun, a pitiful anonymity, a woman solitary and neglected, sitting by herself at the far corner of a table. Said sits next to her, Said whom she had imagined—only imagined—was in love with her. The thought had made her happy, because she wanted to imagine that someone was in love with her. Said smiles and laughs as he exchanges pleasantries with friends and neighbors. She eats slowly, mechanically, never taking her eyes off the hamburger on her paper plate. She smiles absently as the memory of Angele and the halva sandwich comes floating back to her. She wonders if she's turning into a version of Angele, a plump woman with short hair, crushed by fear, seeking out imaginary walls to flatten herself against. Pluto is facing her down for the next few years after all. The house she grew up in, the familiar houses of neighbors, have vanished into the thin air of time. Her only vista now is the endless corridor of Flatbush Avenue twisting and turning into alien side streets.

She leaves just as she had come. She gets into the car with Said. She notices that he seems unusually cheerful.

"How come you're in such a good mood?" she asks him timidly.

"I'm always happy, as my name says."

"How lucky for you."

"If a person has faith, they'll always be happy."

She feels like she's heard this before. She's heard it a lot, heard it and even repeated it herself many times. But she feigns innocence, to please him.

"Faith in what?" she asks stupidly.

"In God of course."

She worries that he's about to start preaching to her in earnest by the look on his face. She suddenly realizes that he has prepared his catechism in advance, thinking to change her life, to save her from herself, but she alone knows that in this lesson lies her destruction. She struggles to evoke a cord of empathy with which to bind this stranger to her. She gazes at the vertical scar on his face.

"Do you know that you're the first man to ask me out in this city?" she murmurs wistfully. She hopes to soften his heart and to make him see her as a woman.

He smiles and avoids her eyes.

She continues: "I want to feel free tonight. Free from expectations of any kind. Free to save myself in my own way, free to be myself. Do you know what that means?"

She laughs and throws her head back coyly on the passenger seat of the limousine, but he doesn't say anything. She suggests they take a walk so that she can tell him more, but she's all wound up now; she feels hurt and also offended. She would have thrown herself into his arms if he'd asked her to, would have stayed next to him in the car forever, with no shame. Her excitement is cosmic. Mars has recently moved into her zodiac, adding layers of cruel impetuosity to her usual anxiousness. Said is unmoved. She tells him the story of her grandmother as they sit eating ice cream on Seventh Avenue, but he is restrained and uncomfortable, an insipid smile plastered on his face.

She watches his car move away down the long dark street, then she goes into Coco Bar—the bar below her apartment—and orders a beer. She regrets not having told him her father's story instead: maybe it would have been more effective. She reproaches herself for not having given him the opportunity to be a hero: men have their dream roles too, she muses sadly. Now she feels unbearably heavy with a longing to open up and talk. She looks around her. Most of the customers in the bar are women sitting by themselves, like her. She wonders who listens to the stories spinning around in dusty corners of their brains.

She sees her father sitting on the mat in the eastern balcony surrounded by camphor and tamarisk trees. Noah speaks from his ark to his son who is standing on the mountain that will save him from the deluge. He says, "There is no protection from God's judgment, save for those who have earned his mercy." The eastern balcony lies wide open to the sky. Hend rubs her father's feet. His head lies in her mother's lap. Stars shine down on the circle that her brothers form around him. They're all close to each other in age, except for the oldest, who has grown tall and proud of his small beard. He disappears into God's way for a few days every month and his mother says, "He's studying," because she refuses to believe that the handsome, gentle son who used to collect stamps and play the harmonica and devour comic books has become an Islamist. Little Hend didn't understand why he came up the steps that led up to the eastern balcony with those deliberate, epic strides that day and screamed in her father's face: "Shame on you! It's forbidden—what you're doing is a sin!"

The father raises his head from his wife's lap and sits up. The younger brothers, who were all engrossed in the story of Noah, look at each other and then at their big brother. The father taps his knee with his fingers in a silent drumbeat of fury. He doesn't say a word and the oldest son, tall and skinny in his spotlessly white, scented jalaba, runs away, shouting an expression that he's learned by heart: "May God curse the one who drinks it or traffics in it or buys it." He hides in the pantry and cries alone among the sacks piled up in the corners and the odor of moldy wheat. He cries like a small, terrified child. "I'm afraid that he'll go to hell, mother. You know how much I love him." The father withdraws into his room, leaning on little Hend's shoulder. "Are you sad, Papa?" she asks him. He doesn't reply. He lies down on his bed and turns on the small radio on the nightstand to listen to the BBC news bulletin.

She massages his tired feet as he likes her to do. Her palm is small and frail and comforting. With each stroke she tries to dissipate the unnatural fog of silence that envelops him. The mother comes in leading her oldest son, still crying, by the hand. The father smiles when he sees him, then he suddenly bursts out laughing as though just at that moment discovering that this young man is his firstborn child. The son hangs his head and says, "I'm afraid for you, Papa." The father smiles. "The mountain will save me from the waters." The son replies with a practiced formula to prove his claim: "'That thing of which much intoxicates is forbidden even in the smallest quantity.'" The father smiles again. "'A little of it strengthens the heart and does away with sorrow.' Do you know who said that? The famously strict jurist Ahmad ibn Hanbal. Which means that you're more of a Hanbali than Ibn Hanbal himself." The eldest son cries and the father laughs. He's found his sense of humor again now, and he insists that beer is "a great pharaonic invention." Then he goes to sleep, complaining of a pain in his left shoulder.

Many years later, his daughter sits in a small bar in a neighborhood of Brooklyn. She stares at the foam in her glass, the white bubbles popping as they settle on its surface. The pretty young bartender looks at her sympathetically. She asks about her son. "Where's the cute little man I always see you with?" Hend smiles at the question and points to the ceiling of the bar, above which the boy lies on his bed waiting for her to come home.

Hend sleeps a lot because she is always tired, because she is all alone, and because she doesn't have anything particular to do. She pulls the covers over her face to hide her exhaustion from him. He snuggles up to her as he watches drawn faces like her own talking on the TV screen. "The signs of depression are constant fatigue, irritability, apathy, feelings of sadness, and suicidal thoughts. Ask your doctor about treatment. Depression is painful. Ask your doctor about Cymbalta. Cymbalta can help." He watches the faces in the commercial as they materialize and then fade into nothing. He shakes her under the covers. "Mom, sometimes you don't answer me when I talk to you and you act sad—*very sad*," he repeats in English.

"So?" she asks wearily.

"You should go see a doctor. You might die!"

"Don't worry."

"But if you do die for example, what would happen to me?"

"You'd go back to Egypt."

"But I don't want to go back to Egypt."

"We have to go back sometime."

"Why do we have to? If you're not happy here you could take Cymbalta, or go to the doctor."

She buries her head in the pillow and laughs. He doesn't like it when she laughs at him. He turns his face away angrily, and she burrows her head deep under the pillow and goes to sleep.

Tango

She hears his footsteps on the stairs, and wonders how one person can make all that noise. The first time she saw him in the building he was standing on the landing in front of her door. He had tripped over her son's bicycle and dropped the carton of bottles that he was carrying. When she opened the door he was picking up the pieces of broken glass that had scattered all over the landing and cursing the landlord and the tenants and anyone else he could think of. She quietly took her son's bicycle inside and shut the door, leaving him to figure out how to clean up the spilled beer. The smell of alcohol lingered on her floor for a long time after, the smell of hops and beery foam, as well as a few tiny shards of broken glass. The second time he saw her he tried to be more pleasant. He said that the landlord rarely rented apartments to families with children and that he was glad she and her son had moved in—it made the building seem more cheerful. She nodded as she looked at the dark, narrow stairs and breathed in the strong wood smell that rose from the old banister. As he talked, she looked everywhere but at him, then she quietly went up to her apartment.

He lived in the apartment right above hers. Every time he went up or down the stairs he always had a carton of bottles with him. He wore a baseball cap and rode around on a bicycle that he locked up on the ground floor of the building. He lived alone. She had guessed this from the slow, rhythmic sound of his footsteps tapping above her every night. She got to know the sound of his hurried steps on the stairs too, what time he went to work, and what time he came back. She knew that he eavesdropped on the tenants with those sharp ears of his. Whenever she met him on the stairs, he said the same thing: "Did you hear the ruckus in the building yesterday? That band and the loud music? I have no idea why the landlord rents to crazy people like that. I can't sleep in this building! Children, live music, bizarre neighbors . . . ."

She left him cursing and complaining and went into her apartment. She knew for a fact that he had his own share of bizarre visitors, such as that petite woman who came to see him from time to time. She would lock up her bike next to his and climb the stairs with a six-pack of beer. When she came to visit, the loud music moved from the apartment next door to the one upstairs—his apartment—and drowned out the rhythmic noise of their lovemaking. The climax of their sighs and moans floated in and out of the regular, booming beat above her head. She would turn up her TV or the AC but she couldn't sleep until the battle upstairs was finally over. The woman always left at midnight on the dot. She descended the stairs with the empty beer bottles, which she threw in the garbage chute, then took her bike and rode off into the night.

The tiny fair-skinned woman disappeared for days, and sometimes weeks, and then he would enter into a period of absolute silence. During these periods she rarely heard the sound of his footsteps above her, just the rush of water flushing in the toilet or the clanking of pots and pans in the kitchen. She smelled the odor of coffee coming from his open window. She knew that his bed was exactly above her own, and when he tossed and turned she pictured him mumbling restlessly in his sleep.

During these periods of hibernation, Hend turned her attention to her downstairs neighbor. She wove a story out of the young woman's comings and goings and her boyfriend's visits. The smell of tacos drifted up to her from the downstairs window.

Hend drew perverse comfort from the cheerless building. She took pleasure in sharing intimate moments with anonymous, unsuspecting people, people who surely recognized the timbre of her voice when she yelled at her son and the sound of water bubbling and purring in her pipe at night. They knew that she slept alone, and that she talked in her sleep. She always left the TV on at night because she was afraid of the silence. Her next-door neighbors knew her son's name and which school he went to. They saw her crossing the street with him every morning. They knew what time she washed the dishes every day, and recognized the smell of tea with cloves wafting out from her window in the evenings. They knew the sound of her laugh and the nights when insomnia stalked her: the nights when she would lie awake terrified that her heart might suddenly stop beating and that she'd be forced to leave the young boy behind, peacefully asleep in his bed, forever. She imagined him rubbing his eyes awake in the morning, then shaking her cold, rigid body in a growing crescendo of terror. She scrawled the names and numbers of all the people she knew in Brooklyn on the kitchen wall—Emilia, Said, Fatima—and she made sure his passport was visible on the kitchen table. That way anyone could find him and send him to his father. He would simply pick up his passport and go back, leaving her body for the landlord and the police to deal with, and the Refugee Aid Society would toss it into any old cemetery.

She hears footsteps on the old wooden stairwell. She knows they aren't her upstairs neighbor's heavy steps. She recognizes them: they belong to his blonde lady friend. But the tiny woman doesn't keep going up the next flight of stairs to his apartment. She stops at her apartment. Hend waits for the knock, and when she opens the door she notices that the woman's nose is red and swollen. Up close, she looks to be in her late forties or early fifties. She holds a little girl by the hand, about the same age as her own son. "Excuse me for barging in on you like this," she says tersely, as though they've known each other for a long time. "Could I leave my daughter with you for a few minutes? I have to talk to him. I'll be right back." Then she sprints up the stairs. The girl, who seems very wise for her age, steps inside as though being taken in charge by a stranger is the most normal of circumstances, something that happens to her every day. She walks into the room and sits down next to the boy, who is busy watching TV. They don't exchange a word at first. They just sit there and watch the cartoons for a while. Finally, they begin to talk as though they had been sitting on that couch together since the day they were born.

"Do you like SpongeBob?" she asks.

"He's funny."

"I like Iron Man. What about Hannah Montana?"

"Girls always like Hannah Montana. Isn't that silly?"

This minor difference of opinion quickly turns into a sharp exchange accompanied by an anxious swinging of legs, and words like "dumb," "stupid," and "freaky" fly around the room. They were two kids who had never laid eyes on each other before, then suddenly discovered that they were sharing a couch, and decided to make the best of it.

She was still observing them intently when the knock came again at the door. The tiny blonde woman was back. Her nose was red from crying and there was no mistaking the miserable expression on her face. She spoke in the same neutral tone. "Excuse me again. Can you call my daughter? Thanks." The girl left quietly, just as she had come. They descended the narrow wooden staircase together and disappeared forever. She never saw her going up or coming down again, or heard her athletic body bouncing on the bed right above her head. Her upstairs neighbor's movements grew slower than usual. Even the sound of running water in his bathroom trickled into nothing. She wondered whether he had moved out of the building altogether or killed himself. Utter silence reigned above the ceiling of her room. It took him a long time to return to his normal self. She started seeing him again as she led her son by the hand to school. She would see him parking his bike downstairs and carrying the six-pack of beer up to his apartment late at night.

Sometimes they'd meet by chance and he would nod at her briefly. Once in a while he'd say a few words like, "The weather is gorgeous today" or "How's your son? Does he like New York?"

The spring breezes pass over Flatbush Avenue and her son spends more and more of his time playing chess and watching Iron Man and SpongeBob on TV. Every evening, for an hour or so, she sits outside the building on the wooden bench in front of Coco Bar, right opposite Mr. Falafel, and watches the world go by on the broad avenue. The bench was frequented by smokers and dog-walkers, or joggers catching their breath after a long run. She sits alone and watches the passersby, drinking coffee and smoking her cigarette. Her upstairs neighbor passes by and stops to chat. "Do you like to dance? Have you ever tried tango or salsa?" She gets the impression that he's asking her out on a date. She sees his face up close for the first time. He looked to be about sixty, but the setting sun makes him look older in spite of his tall, athletic build. She tries to smile in response to his friendly question. "I'd like to, but I've never had the chance. I didn't even dance on my wedding day. I sat on a chair and watched my husband dance with every one of my friends." He chuckles at this, and she realizes that there's more to him than meets the eye. She finds out that his name is Charlie. "There are schools for dancing, you know." He hands her a card and says that he's a dance instructor and that he'd be happy to give her some lessons—for free of course. She nods her head. "All right, maybe," she murmurs. She was tired of watching other people living. She decides that maybe it's time to start coloring her hair again and getting out a bit.

The first time she went to the spacious dance studio with the gleaming parquet floor she felt a thrill at seeing her face, smiling and happy, reflected back at her in so many mirrors. She stared at the body that was a stranger to her. Ever since the day of her first period, her body has been an obscure question mark. Unlike her girlfriends, the onset of puberty came relatively late for her. In class the girls talked about their cramps and the flow of blood and compared the size of their growing breasts. Hend always tried to make herself invisible in these gatherings; she pretended total indifference even though she had memorized the entire chapter on reproductive anatomy in her biology textbook. The biology teacher said, "I'm not going to explain this particular lesson in class. Read it at home." The girls giggled in low voices. The drawings of the male reproductive organs in the book astonished and frightened them. The chapter was at the very end of the book, after the chapters on the digestive, respiratory, and nervous systems. It was appended to the chapter on cell division. Normal everyday words took on unprecedented sexual meanings: 'the tube'; 'the socket'; 'male and female.' But the words that unsettled Hend most were the ones that came from her geography book: innocent words like 'topography' and 'plains and valleys' suddenly began to give off the smell of sex. She quickly discovered that she was the only one of her classmates who hadn't yet been visited by 'the sculptor of girls'—that master craftsman of folk legend who chisels out the curves of waists and breasts and bellies and buttocks, adding a touch here and there to the planes of the face, along with a smattering of pimples.

When her period finally came, it was brown, like coffee, just a few dark spots she discovered in her underpants. Later, it was like rivers of dark red blood, and she had to use loads of those cloth rags that her mother kept hidden in the bathroom (this was before the invention of disposable sanitary napkins). A single swollen pimple appeared on the tip of her nose every month. It would come and then go, and her body would go back to normal, her face resuming its placid roundness. She began to develop a new relationship with her bodily fluids. She became obsessed with fantastic love stories and poems about solitude and longing and passionate embraces. She took perverse pleasure in the explosive fits of weeping that came over her, and in contemplating the mysterious rhythms produced by her hormones and the pimples full of watery pus. She did not love her body and she had never thought about it much before. She came to understand that the violent emotions that seized her were cyclic, tied to the paired ebb and flow of hormones and planets. Hers was a water sign: she was born to be curious, timid, dreamy, and delusional. It was a pretty hopeless sign all in all despite its tendency to selflessness and empathy.

Hend's periods stopped when she was thirty-three years old, for reasons that she only understood later. On a day like all the others, she came out of her bedroom holding the baby's bottle, the baby who slept curled in a ball between them on the bed that smelled of talcum powder and saliva, of urine and sweat and vomit, of medicines for fever and indigestion. The bedspread was covered with stains, and patches of desiccated milk spotted her blouse. She went into the kitchen and put the water and anise leaves in the kettle. As she waited for the tea to boil she wandered into his study and began to poke around in his open desk drawer. Her hand immediately fell upon a packet of letters. All she remembers now from those letters are a few passionate phrases that he had written to some woman or other. The baby began to cry, the tea boiled over, and the milk in her breast burned. She went back into the bedroom and tore up the letters into tiny pieces over his sleeping, twitching body, then she began to hit him with both her hands. "Get up! Get out! I don't want to see you in this house ever again."

So he left, and then he came back with angry excuses. The 'lapse' became a string of repeated lapses, and they ceased to shock her. The bouts of hysterical weeping turned to stony silence, and the silence to repulsion. Then the repulsion became a hard, resigned detachment. It was during this time that her periods became shorter and less frequent, and Hend discovered that the sticky liquid—that irritating guest—was deeply connected to her body's well-being, much like the milk that seeped out from her nipples at inexplicable and inconvenient times.

The dance studio is paneled with mirrors. She can see her body clearly in them. She ponders the old scar underneath her eyes, the one that used to make her feel shy all the time, the one that she was always trying to hide in her childhood. She would stand in front of the mirror and place her hand on her cheek to erase it from the image in the glass. She tried yogurt and honey face masks, and all kinds of exfoliating creams. After each experiment, the image looking back at her from the mirror would be sharper. She pored over the beauty pages in magazines and diligently researched the best concealing foundations. In later years it became more pronounced, like a scabby wound stamped on her cheek right under the eye, an area that all the beauty experts warned was especially sensitive. Every year, she would note with surprise that the scar had gotten worse, and that, as the wrinkles accumulated on her face, it became a broad convex arc. She told herself sardonically that it was her very own beauty mark and that it made her face unforgettable.

And she actually began to believe it. She took to decorating it with a tiny penciled mole—a mole like the one the voluptuous actress Mimi Shakib wore in old Egyptian movies, a perfectly round mole that looked like a stain spreading miserably inside the scar. She rubbed in more foundation creams and thought about getting it surgically removed. Maybe she would get a nose job and collagen injections for her lips while she was at it. Perhaps she should pluck her eyebrows to give them a nice high arch. That would mean she'd have to change the color of her hair and her contact lenses too. Her dreams of a brand new body never materialized, of course. Her belly grew big with the baby and she spent all her time after that chasing after the crawling infant and feeding him and poring over the resemblance between his little face and her grown one: the same receding upper lip, the same slightly prominent nose and thick eyebrows joined at the middle. He would put his hand on her scar and ask, "What's this, Mama?" When she hugged him she discovered that the curve of his spine and his fingers were shaped exactly like hers. Her child feels her scar with his palm and kisses it, then runs off to grow up on his own, leaving her behind. She frets about her body's other imperfections—the flabby flesh around her stomach, the muscles grown flaccid from pregnancy and childbirth.

She examines her body as though she's never seen it before. She ponders its little scars and defects, all more noticeable now in the short dress she's wearing: stitches in the knee after falling off a swing at her uncles' house, a break in the right arm when she climbed the gate of their house in one of her attempts to escape, a burn on the back of her hand from the first time she fried potatoes, droopy eyelids from plucking the brows over and over, rolls of flesh around the stomach that used to be tightly knit bands of muscle holding him firmly in place when he was a fetus, the old scar under her eye. She watches her face moving through all those mirrors: features stripped of all their usual veils, wrinkled by the months and years, leaving Hend with this profound feeling that her life is now all behind her.

Charlie took her by the hand and began to teach her the first step: "One, two, three, four." He was unusually tall and he didn't move like an old man at all. His body was sinewy and graceful. She turned in circles a few times, getting her steps mixed up, not knowing where to look—at her feet or at the mirrors? Or at his face? He moved between the students in the group, pulling them close to him one by one, as though they were all his lovers: "One, two, three, four." Everyone settled into the rhythmic movements—she was the only one who kept making the same mistakes, and the knowledge of it made her even more confused and clumsy. The dance seemed to her like a string of mistakes repeated with the same obstinate stupidity. It was exactly like her life: a game in which two people came together and moved apart according to strict rules regulating momentum and balance. She couldn't quite grasp the requisite equilibrium and she stumbled again and again. She had never liked the game in real life and she didn't like it as a formal dance either. She just couldn't bring herself to let a man take her by the hand and hold her in his arms, and she couldn't believe that all she had to do was to respond slowly and gracefully. A step back and a step forward. She turned in helpless circles and lost her balance. She suspected that they were all laughing at her.

She tried to watch what the other dancers were doing. She felt ashamed of the smell of sweat coming from her armpits. She wondered whether the bulkiness of her torso made her less agile. Her legs were too stiff to execute the sudden dips and twirls properly and she suddenly felt infinitely tired.

After class she walked back home with Charlie. As they talked, she got the strange feeling that she'd met him before. Here, away from the dance floor, he reminded her of a frog—of all the men in her life that she had never really liked. She wondered at the chameleon-like nature of men. She remembered the first time she actually saw her husband cheating on her. She hated that word, 'cheating.' It made her think of old Zahrit al-Ula movies. Zahrit al-Ula always played the role of the tearful, deceived wife who lived in the shadows and talked a lot about virtue and self-respect. Hend detested the wife role: real heroines were never wives. Mistresses in movies were a lot more appealing. They had plunging necklines and wide, glittering eyes that could hold a gaze without blinking. But Hend began to doubt that she had ever been suited for the role of leading lady. She just wasn't qualified. That's why her favorite old movie was *The Well of Privation*, where the heroine committed every kind of sin in her dreams at night, then woke up in the morning fresh and unsullied.

She told Charlie all about the first time she saw her husband flirting with another woman. It happened in her own house and the woman was her friend. All his mistresses were her friends—or plotted to become her friends after the fact. She still didn't understand what the point was. She remembers the evening clearly. She was wearing a pretty new dress and moving gaily around the room, full of that glowing self-assurance that only fools live on. The guests were heatedly discussing something—what, she can't recall. She didn't know any of their faces, had never seen them before. Her husband meanwhile was engaged in a different type of conversation. Her friend had been dancing alone to an old Umm Kulthum song. Hend had always loved that particular melody and they often listened to it together as the friend told her stories about the early days of her first marriage and her life since. She sat down opposite Hend's husband and they began to steal long, languorous glances at each other. It wasn't difficult for Hend to see that her husband knew this woman well, that he had handled her body and whispered to her in the arrogant and lewd accents of masculine possession. Hend was as good at reading these signs and tokens as she was at stuffing cabbage leaves or pigeons and making rice casseroles. She was like Zahrit al-Ula in the old movies. She watched the brazen, defiant exchange that dared everyone to notice. They could all see what was going on right in front of their noses. But people like to share in little conspiracies. The truth remains unsaid and the unsaid is, when all's said and done, immaterial.

Hend recalls the scene unfolding. Her friend went over to the buffet and her husband followed her and picked at the hors d'oeuvres. Then his hand reached out to stroke the cleft between her breasts, and she shivered and laughed nervously. Hend was just coming out of the kitchen with a tray of finger food, but she pretended that she hadn't seen anything. She just turned around and walked straight back into the kitchen. "The way of the world," she whispered to herself, just as her mother had taught her. It's true that this had all happened rather early in her married life, but what did that matter? All men were the same, weren't they? It was the first time her husband had appeared repulsive and obscene to her, and also the first time that she felt unbearably stupid and terribly slow. Incidents like these multiplied and the snapshots she stored in her head became clearer and sharper. The violent confrontations grew more frequent—confrontations in which he always denied everything, because denial is the fuel of conspiracy. He accused her of being crazy. Hend turned in circles frantically looking for his missing underwear and socks. She spent her days searching for proof of his infidelities, but whenever she found something, pretending that everything was fine became that much harder and her need to flee that much more urgent. She began to avoid him entirely.

In the beginning she took her frustration out on the pillows as though they alone were the cause of her misery. She went through terrible mood swings—shrinking from his body in disgust and then making passionate love to him. She began to hate the mattress that they slept on. It had belonged to him before they married, and those dark stains and musty smells had not been made by her. Yes, she knew the way of the world now: knew, as her mother had taught her, that a man's only disgrace was the size of his wallet, and yet she clung fiercely to her madness. She stitched up a brand new clean white cotton mattress that she could call her own, and tossed and turned on it with her heavy, bloated belly.

Charlie listened to her without a word. Did he even understand what she was saying? Maybe her accent was too thick. Or maybe he just wasn't interested. She started to tell him about her nightmares.

She sees her friends, and sometimes the men she's secretly loved, clasping hands and forming a circle around her. Each one tries to touch her in turn. The game is called 'blind bear.' She is the only person wearing a blindfold; she is the dimwitted one. She runs panting after the shadows that form in the inky darkness. The blind bear turns around and around, frantically searching for the hands that push her from behind. She cocks her ear to catch the loud voices that surround her. She whirls her stick in the air to measure the empty space. She tries to avoid the groping hands that seek her. They push her and she falls, over and over. The game ends when she finally begs for mercy. They make a circle around her and taunt her: "The blind bear's fallen into the well!" The well is deep and her fall is exhilarating. She falls, over and over, endlessly. She always wakes up from this dream in utter panic. The blind bear is dimwitted and makes the same mistakes over and over. She falls in love with the same man over and over. She believes that all she has to do is bend so as not to break. It's hard for her to say these things to Charlie because she doesn't know how to translate them into his language. She hopes he has understood.

She could hear the sound of water splashing on her husband's body in the bathroom. She pictured his naked body moving around as he shaved and picked out his clothes. He sang in his room. He sang with the pure delight of a man in love. She waited till she heard the front door shut behind him before coming out from her room to take a warm bath. She breathed a sigh of relief. She decided that she wouldn't even bother to tell him that she was leaving on a trip and maybe never coming back, and that she didn't love him any more — that his presence in this world wounded her. She wished that she could force him to take off his clothes — the clothes that smelled of another woman — before he came into her house. Sometimes she sniffed them all over for that smell. But she didn't care in the end; she just wanted to know the truth, to convince herself that she had plumbed his depths. She knew where he hid his letters and when he came in his dreams as she lay sleeping next to him. She was quite familiar with the sticky, foul-smelling stains on his underwear and she understood why he was always leaving them around for her to find. She knew why he always kept his cell phone close to him, in his pocket or under his pillow at night. On that day he had forgotten it on the edge of the dresser. She turned the sleeping phone over in her hands as she waited for the tub to fill with water. She stood there for a long time, lost in thought, then decided to turn it on and read the messages. She still experienced a feeling of utter panic at moments like these. The clean, warm water caressed her body. The phone beckoned. She knew that the PIN code was made up of the letters of her name. After a few tries she got the right combination and scrolled through to the inbox with its long list of messages. She already knew what she would find there: promised kisses, obscene whispers, and postponed meetings. She drowned the phone in the bathwater to erase its memory once and for all.

Charlie patted her shoulder and smiled sympathetically, then he gave her a quick kiss on the cheek and ran up the stairs to his apartment.

The women taking classes with Hend at the dance studio dressed in long, flowery skirts like the ones Zahrit al-Ula wore in the movies. They clutched scented handkerchiefs and wore high-heeled shoes. Each woman seemed to turn in circles around her own failures. The music was always sad, and the lyrics were about weeping women and the men who abandoned them. The sticky, sweaty palms of her dance partners left her cold and unmoved. At the end of the lesson everybody turned their backs on everybody else and walked off in different directions. Charlie stayed behind with her only because they lived in the same building and he felt obliged to walk her home. As they walked next to each other, he told her that he started dancing after his first divorce because he wanted to learn how to gauge the proper distance between a man and a woman; to learn the exact point of balance between desire and retreat, intimacy and habit. Hend nodded her head. She had never danced with a man before. When Charlie danced he seemed much younger than he really was, and as he talked she could hardly believe that he was the same man who dragged his bike along angrily every morning, cursing the building and its tenants. He explained the history of the dance to her. He told her that it began with the first wail unleashed by the prisoners in the slave ships, then its rhythms were picked up by the Spaniards who crossed the seas. It was the same lecture he gave all his students. She realized nonetheless that he was deliberately trying to be charming as she walked by his side demurely. When he put his arm around her, her unexpectedly firm reply surprised her. "I hope you don't mind my saying this, but please don't do that." Did he understand? Did he put her rejection of him down to some kind of radical cultural difference? She left a wider space between them now as they walked: that hypothetical distance that he was always talking about in class, a distance that begs for uncomplicated sympathy.

Charlie told her that the tango is a dance of longing. She liked this way of putting it. "Why do you love me?" she had once asked her first love long ago (a question that women often ask to gauge the measure of their uniqueness in their lover's eyes). "Do you know that Fairuz song?" he replied, "I'm Yearning for Someone Whose Face

I've Never Seen"? That was all he said. He left her to translate and she came to the conclusion that, as far as he was concerned, their relationship was nothing but the whisper of an obscure longing, like the longing of Charlie's Spaniards. Back then his words had wounded her deeply, but she later realized that this vague, objectless longing was also part of the way of the world. The other women in the dance studio were living examples of this dictum. They had crossed over gently into their thirties. Little wrinkles had begun to sprout at the edges of their faces. She could see them sitting, like her, at windows overlooking some avenue or other, calmly watching life pass by and aching to become a part of it. The tango was a kind of therapy that helped them understand the basic rules of love and life, rules whose time was slowly expiring: distance, attraction, and balance.

The dance resembles the game of love. The world retreats as the partner moves in, then rushes forward again as he turns his back and moves away with choreographed steps. The act of coming together and moving apart precisely and deliberately creates an exact distance between solitary bodies that is the notional space of union. The man approaches this space cautiously. He gently reaches out and takes the woman's hand in his with confidence and desire. "Relax in his embrace. Let him lead you. Let him decide when to pull you close and push you away in a single, graceful movement." The tango, Charlie says, is the philosophy of shared space. She discovers that most of the other students, both men and women, have been recently divorced; the question of distance perplexes them too.

The second time that she and Charlie walked home together she felt the need to talk and talk. She felt that she had gotten to know him better, that his face had grown familiar to her. It no longer reminded her of a frog's face. Now he looked more like a greyhound, with slender, well-proportioned limbs made for running races, or a fantastic creature in an animated film. He reminded her of herself too, because he was alone and wretched just like her, crushed by the noise of a building in which other people made love as he lay alone in bed at night, listening. He held out a glass of white wine to her and they sat down on the bench opposite the Coco Bar. The air was hot. His forehead was wet with perspiration and she could feel it staining the underarms of her blouse. She told him that she was a Cancer. "Do you know that Cancer is notoriously bad at finding its balance?" She told him that Cancers were like the blind bear, falling in love for no reason. Cancers also like to close their eyes and run after their one true love. As a child she was really good at playing hide-and-seek, running, running away, then finding herself standing all alone, hiding in the shade of a wall. No one ever noticed that she was gone and the game always ended with or without her. It pained her. It still pains her. She told him how she had always wanted to write, but that her memory was no longer as good as it used to be, and that she had begun to forget everything. He drank more wine because maybe it would help him understand what this woman who lived under his bed was saying to him. He wiped away the sweat from his forehead more than once. The smell of alcohol and perspiration drifted out of his open mouth and he started to pant for breath like an amateur horseman. She began telling him enthusiastically about her other childhood games, for example her very favorite game: Open This Door for Me.

She stands in the very middle of a circle made by the children, defenseless and exposed. The children clasp hands and tug at each other with interlaced fingers. The circle draws in and expands out in surging waves. In the middle stands the victim. She is the victim, both pathetic and belligerent. She declares war on the joined arms that surround her. In an attempt to break the siege she dashes forward like a sacrificial offering that has torn loose from its tether. Her blood boils and her face grows red, she is like a bull driven to frenzy by the hand of the matador. "Open this door for me!" The singsong reply follows: "The ox has given birth!" The frenzied beast fears that they'll steal her calf away so better not open the door and let her escape. The arms, joined in a spiraling circle, draw closer and closer around her body. When they got a little older the words of the chorus changed to "Open your eyes, flower; close your eyes, flower." She turns and turns like a bee dropping into the stamen of a flower. She searches for a way out of the circle that represents the delicate petals of a flower devouring its victim. The girls abandon her one by one.

Charlie grew tired of listening to her. His face took on a bored, knowing expression. "I understand completely. I understand how you feel." He said it to stem the flow of pointless memories. Charlie didn't realize that loneliness was to blame; a desperate need to connect to just about anybody, even to a person with the face of a frog and a body that gave off the odor of sweat and lust and expediency.

As he climbed the narrow stairway, he grabbed her hand and started to pull her up behind him to the room that lay right above her son's head, her son who was probably poring over his map of Africa at that very moment. Charlie's eyes were bloodshot from fatigue and from listening to her endless stories. He popped open a bottle of beer and lit a cigarette, then he pounced on her, his hands creeping over the bare skin exposed by her low-cut dress. She told him simply that she couldn't sleep with him because she didn't love him. She said it as succinctly as possible: "I don't love you." She shivered as she said it, like a blood-red sea crab just emerged from the water. He had tried to convince her of the truth that love and hate mean nothing in the dance as in life, and that all she had to do was relax the muscles of her mind and give her body a chance to express itself, but Hend wasn't convinced. The fragile spell cast by the wine and the circle of dancers was broken and Charlie went back to being a clay frog of a man she didn't love. She knew that he wanted her to be like that other woman, the one who left her daughter at Hend's apartment out of the blue one day. She dodged his stifling arms and ran away. She heard him slam the door behind her and mutter expressively: "Big fat ass." Exhausted, she cried alone in her room.

Now she worried more about her big fat ass than her dance steps and she made even more stupid mistakes, turning around and around in halting circles, desperately trying to imitate the other women. He would take her hand doggedly as though he were training an obstinate mule: "One, foot forward, two, together, three, backward . . . ." She concentrated on her high-heeled shoes and moved her feet carefully but she still couldn't get it right. "Don't look at your feet," he yells at her. "Here," he points to his eyes, "look here." She knows what men are like when they get tired of a woman. They get just the way Charlie did when he put his hand around her waist impatiently and twirled her in a lumbering, clumsy circle. Suddenly he stood perfectly still and said in front of everyone, "I'm not going to eat you. No one in this world intends to eat you, I can promise you that. This is just a dance, my dear." She pulled away from him and stood alone, staring at her crooked feet in the mirror. But he wasn't finished. "My dear, you have to leave your inhibitions at the door and give your body a chance to express itself." He said this in the calm and professional tone of a dance instructor, but her face turned red with mortification and her heart began to thump in her chest. He spent the rest of the lesson focusing on the other middle-aged women as they moved about nimbly. Hend decided that dancing was not for her. Neither was love for that matter, or anything that she had ever set her heart on. Later, she watched him cross the street, jump onto his bike, and disappear down Seventh Avenue. She walked back alone through the dark streets that led to her house.

From then on they carefully avoided each other. Her friend Fatima, who had also taken a few classes at his studio, started to pay him visits at home. Hend would hear the sound of her perfectly formed rear end going up and down the stairs. She never stopped to knock at Hend's door and say hello or tell her what she was doing up there. Only the scent of Hend's clove tea floated up to them in the evening, while the smell of his cigarettes and the rustle of their whispers floated down through the window that exposed her little home to the world's indifferent gaze.

Atlantic Avenue

The first thing that Americans do when they wake up in the morning is hurry off to Dunkin' Donuts. The Dunkin' Donuts at the corner of Atlantic and Fourth Avenues is a pale salmon color. The oldest community of Arab-American immigrants lives in the neighborhood. Next door to the Dunkin' Donuts stands a mosque frequented by African-American Muslims, then there's the Yemeni restaurant called Saba, the Brooklyn Islamic Center, and a number of shops that sell miswak toothpicks and musk oil and Qurans and prayer rugs. There's also an old-age home nearby, as well as a homeless shelter, a spa, and a welfare office on Fulton street where the poor go for food stamps and unemployment benefits. Female workers—especially immigrants—are in high demand because their wages are generally lower, and because employers imagine that women of color are better at communicating with customers who look like them, customers who can understand their heavy accents and argue comfortably about pennies counted out with vigilance.

She leaves him sleeping deeply. She resents the thought of him waking up in an empty apartment, getting dressed by himself, struggling over his shoelaces. She won't know for sure whether he's wrapped his scarf tight around his neck against the biting cold or whether he'll be safe crossing the street alone and walking to school with no one to watch over him. She panics whenever she sees a poster of a missing child. A sharp needle of grief pricks her heart because she knows he has to grow up and become a man without any help from her. She's afraid for him. She gazes at his round, healthy cheeks and wide black eyes and the broad smile that he bestows upon friends and strangers alike. She is constantly warning him about passersby and neighbors and strangers and schoolmates older than him, about teachers and classrooms and the school bathrooms and football tackles. She tried to explain to him that he was a little man already, that he must never let any other man touch him, whether in affection or anger, but she couldn't be sure that he understood her. "Fine," he would reply impatiently, and again, in English: "Fine."

But that didn't ease her fear. She was afraid when she hurried down the street in the dark just before dawn and hopped onto an empty bus, and she was afraid when she walked alone from the bus stop to the Dunkin' Donuts in front of which knots of people huddled in the early hours of the morning, trying to force their eyes open with a cup of hot black coffee. She changed her clothes quickly in front of Fatima (who didn't resemble her in the least). Fatima was much younger than her, a dark-skinned Somali girl in her late twenties, tall and slender. Her body was flawless, not an ounce of flab, no traces of childbirth or abuse, and her kinky African hair was cut close to her head like a beautiful boy's. Fatima worked the cash register. She was the exact type of woman that the customers liked. She colored her hair white blond, which created a sharp contrast with her small, childish features and shining black skin, and gave her face a kind of electric sensuality. Fatima was born to be a leading lady. She stood there behind the counter and moved her nimble fingers between the bills and the Styrofoam cups of coffee with a sweet, tranquil smile hovering on her lips. "Would you like anything else? Do you want it black or with cream and sugar? Skim milk or whole?" Then she wished you a nice day—sometimes a beautiful day—but sometimes she just smiled that quizzical, tender smile that made the customer feel like an old and cherished friend. They came back again and again on cold, rainy winter mornings because they were addicted to the radiance of her face. Hend's role unfolded, as usual, behind the scenes. She wiped away the coffee stains and arranged the donuts in neat rows and mopped the floor quite gracefully—but no one ever noticed of course. She was constantly on the move between toilets and tables, sometimes distracted and absentminded, other times frowning and pensive.

She spends the whole morning mopping the dirty salmon floor. She stoops slightly as she moves from one table to another. Her rump sticks out, round and strapping, the posterior of a Middle Eastern woman who spends all her time sitting in the same place. Some of the women watch it approvingly as she vigorously attacks the dirty tables. The men are usually drawn to Fatima, no matter what she's doing: frowning, daydreaming, baring her small white teeth in a grin that sets off her full lips. In the morning the workers come, followed by the students. When it starts to rain, the homeless people drift in from all over and greet each other as though they'd made appointments to meet in that very place. They scrupulously count out the round coins in their dirty pockets and then they stand in a long line to order coffee. All day they drag their carts piled high with bric-a-brac: old clothes and shoes, discarded bits of odds and ends, food and drink and blankets. Their shoes are caked in the mud of the surrounding streets and the air fresheners inside aren't enough to dissipate the powerful odor that comes off their skin in waves. They look at her shyly as though asking permission to sit down in peace for a while until the rain stops, and they sit there in proud silence as they tuck their ragged clothes out of sight under their coats. She passes between them to wipe down the tables. They hide inside the close warmth of the place. Dunkin' Donuts is a twenty-four-hour refuge for them, as it is for foreigners with big dreams that are always just out of reach.

She presses her nose against the glass window and watches the snow cover the streets. She starts thinking about him again. Why does God create mothers? Is he running through the playground now? Will he fall and break something on the slippery ground? Will the other kids make fun of his accent? Has he found someone to talk to, or is he still standing alone with his back to the wall like the other immigrant kids? Has he understood that sticking out your middle finger at someone is an obscene gesture, and that it's meant as a grave insult? Do the other kids give him the finger to test his cultural competence?

She moves away from the window and picks up her mop again. She sprays air freshener in the bathrooms to dissipate the oppressive winter air.

Fatima takes her shirt off in front of Hend in the bathroom where they change into their uniforms. Little red spots cover her back and neck. She scratches her skin ferociously, then gently rubs in layers of ointment before carefully putting on her clothes. Hend asks her about the inflamed pimples. "Bedbugs," she replies in disgust. "Haven't you heard of them? Don't you know what they are?" She tells Hend that bedbugs live in the folds of your mattress and come out at night to suck your blood. She says that they feed on the blood of their sleeping victims, and that they reproduce a thousand times every night. They're entirely resistant to pesticides and repellents, they burrow into wood and stick to clothes, and the only way to get rid of them is to burn everything. Hend never knows where Fatima sleeps. Sometimes she spends the night at "John's house," other times at some other man's place. She doesn't like anyone to ask her about the pimples, or about the men, or about Somalia. She dreams of becoming another Naomi Campbell because she's got a tall slender graceful figure that hints of faraway countries, just like her.

They walk next to each other down the streets that the two of them have come to know like the backs of their hands. Sometimes she sits alone for a couple of hours on a wooden chair in front of a washing machine owned by one of the religious Yemenis. He always greets Hend modestly in the Islamic manner—*asalamu 'alaikum*—then turns his face away from Fatima's leotard-clad body. They sit together and puff on the cigarettes that they've been postponing since early morning. Fatima never talks about herself. She isn't like the other immigrants who love to chatter and gossip and invent stories to fill up the blank spaces in their lives. Hend knows that Fatima only hangs around with her so that she can spend the night at her place every once in a while when she needs to get away from her ex-boyfriend John. There isn't much spare room in Hend's studio, so when Fatima sleeps over she has to lay a mattress on the only available floor space in front of the kitchenette. Fatima races up the many flights of stairs, bursts into the apartment, and immediately heads for the shower. She gives her body up to the pulsing water (maybe it will heal those spots on her back). She spends most of her time at Hend's house showering and rubbing lotions into her skin and watching the world go by from the only window in the apartment. She offers Hend advice about her son as he sits quietly drawing his map of Africa: "This kid is going to stay stuck to you like that forever. You should leave him to me—I'll take care of him." She plays chess with him sometimes—a game the boy has discovered a talent for.

Fatima was even more beautiful than Naomi Campbell but nobody seemed to want to discover her. Maybe this was why she wrapped herself tightly in the blanket at night, covered her face in the same way Hend did, and tossed and turned endlessly: another solitary, pitiful woman in the house. Hend drew a little comfort from the likeness. She too liked to press up against windows and dream. At first Hend believed that Fatima was her friend and that she came over to keep her company. Then she realized that she was just looking for a free ride, that she wasn't a friend after all, and this made Hend feel even lonelier. A friend is someone who freely gives sympathy and understanding and this was exactly what Fatima was unable to give. She was too preoccupied with her pimples and her skin and her obscure future.

Hend lived in a world of her own too. She often thought about her old friends and realized that they had been few and far between. She had never been very sociable, or vivacious and amusing. She put this down to her timid, introverted birth sign. Nobody could penetrate the tough outer skin that she hid beneath. At school she sat between Noha and Hanan, Noha on her right and Hanan on her left. Noha's woman-body blossomed quickly but she still liked to play with Hend. Her favorite game of all was hopscotch and she was always playing it on the sidewalk in front of her father's shop. When her dress flew up as she jumped from square to square, Hend could see the inflamed spoon marks on her thighs. Noha loved hopscotch. She would carefully draw the squares with a piece of chalk, pull up her dress, fling out her shapely white legs, and relentlessly pursue the pebble as it skipped from square to square with astonishing speed. A group of boys from the Muqawi School always stopped to stare at her bare legs as they passed by, and she would pull up her dress even further, not caring one bit about the consequences. Keeping her legs raised high for as long as possible was the first womanly skill that Noha had acquired and her talent began to capture the attention of passersby who would stop to watch her skipping from square to square in wonder. Then her furious mother would pull her away by the hair and drag her inside.

Their house was made up of two rooms behind the small shop owned by Noha's father, Amm Mahmud the grocer. Noha watched as her mother took off her dress and a plump woman called Fatma al-Qarumiya proceeded to rub her tired back with a paste made of olive oil and plaster. Fleshy, dark-skinned Fatma al-Qarumiya massaged her back as she sat on a rush mat in the airless room. Her hand slid down from the top of her spinal cord to the compact base of her torso while Noha eavesdroped on the advice she gave her mother as she relaxed into the massage. "So what, seven girls? Your eldest is a boy—what more does he want from you? Another boy? Hmph. That's all he needs! How on earth is Mahmud the grocer going to support all those male kids he's constantly dreaming about having?"

Noha's mother slapped her cheek pitifully. "But he says he's going to get married, Auntie!"

Fatma al-Qarumiya grabbed hold of the woman's naked legs. "Listen to me . . . raise your legs." She depilated the triangle between her thighs with caramelized sugar, then rubbed some oil into it. When she had finished, she sagely nodded her head, which was decorated with two bird tattoos like the ones the gypsies have. "All men are sons of bitches, you silly woman. They're like dogs, hanging on to the world by their cocks." She said this with the wisdom of a woman who had known all kinds of men in her long life, a woman who had achieved complete harmony with the ways of the world.

Noha's mother's skin was loose and flaccid from all those pregnancies and her stomach was bloated with layers of fat and crisscrossed with long stretch marks. Fatma al-Qarumiya slapped the woman's stomach. "Suck that in," she said. Then she pointed to her legs. "Raise those up." She poured a mixture of oil and warm, perfumed water onto them and the dusty ground greedily sucked up the sweet mastic. Noha's mother put on a transparent, open-necked slip printed with pink flowers and decorated with a ribbon around the collar. She smiled, plump and fragrant and ready for the night ahead.

The mother caught her daughter spying on her from behind the half-open door and she pounced on her, pulling her by the hair and pinching her thighs with all the force of her pent-up frustrations. "All day long she plays hopscotch and spreads her legs wide, Auntie. The girl is going to bring calamity down upon me. I've told her over and over, 'Don't you dare spread those legs of yours, girl!'" Noha cried as she told Hend about it, but she kept on playing hopscotch in the schoolyard because she knew that the game brought out all her hidden talents. She drew the squares and spread her legs and skipped ever so gracefully from square to square, and she didn't give a damn that the boys were spying on her. She balanced the pebble on her head, then tossed it with her eyes closed and she skipped away to escape the fate that awaited her mother after the massage of oil and mastic: that moment when she would emerge from the bedroom with wild, unkempt hair and red bruises on her cheeks.

The voice of Noha's father, Amm Mahmud the grocer, follows her—but it's not the gentle and tolerant voice that he uses to bargain with his customers. Now, as he shouts at his wife, it sounds like

91

a fierce, drawn-out hiss. "What are you, a piece of rock, you bitch?" Noha's mother cries and complains of a splitting headache that never leaves her and Fatma al-Qarumiya treats it by engraving a tattoo right where it's tender. Noha meanwhile balanced the pebble on her head and tried to forget what her mother's face looked like as she gathered in her seven daughters on the mat around her and painfully hunched over them like an old rag. Still, she was always ready for her husband because she never knew when he might want her. He shook her by the shoulder some nights and said, "Come."

Noha practiced more and played even harder, so hard that Hend was reduced to watching her friend zip around the court alone, never ever falling or stumbling. Meanwhile, Amm Mahmud the grocer sat in his shop behind the wooden counter that was covered by a filthy stone slab they called "the bank." The women parked their breasts there or plopped down their nursing infants on it as they negotiated with him over the exact number of pennies in their pockets. Sometimes they even came out of these negotiations with a free handful of dried mint or a thin slice of the spun sugar or sesame halva that sat uncovered in the window. The grocer sold cigarettes too, but tobacco wasn't the only thing he rolled into them. 'Satlana'—that which intoxicates the mind—was the other ingredient. "Stuffed or plain?" he asked his customers. The bottles of soda and Stella beer, the barrels of oil and ghee, and the sacks of sugar paled in importance compared to the rolling paper and the hashish cigarettes that were his most profitable source of income. Those townspeople who had gotten rich from the suitcases and money orders coming from Iraq and Yemen and Saudi Arabia were his most valued customers. With the money he made from this trade he built a couple of brick rooms behind his shop and installed an iron gate to prevent his seven daughters from spilling out onto the streets.

Hend stands on the other side of that gate and tries but fails to catch a glimpse of her friend. Noha's mother is the only person in sight. She sits just behind the gate, pulling in the smoke from the water pipe and breathing it out through her nostrils. A fish tattoo decorates her temple and a necklace of plastic fish hangs around her neck along with a few chili peppers: charms against the evil eye that she took to wearing after moving into her new red-brick house. And while it was true that God had blessed them with money, He had cursed her—Umm Noha—with headaches and migraines.

Mahmud the grocer eventually built a second floor made up of two rooms with a stone staircase. He was the first one in town to add another floor to his house, and he painted the upper rooms pink. He began to spread the word of his matrimonial intentions among all the women who leaned up against his 'bank': "I want to get officially married—I swear! The Prophet came to me in a dream and said, 'Mahmud, at least God gave you one son—I only begat girls.' So I said, bless you, I just want another little boy to carry the load, and he replied, 'It's your God-given right, Mahmud.'"

And so Mahmud the grocer married a young, skinny girl in the hope that her back would be stronger and her womb more hospitable than his first wife, and that therefore she would be more likely "to bring the boy to term," as Fatma al-Qarumiya—who knew all about women—advised him. She pulled on the hashish cigarette that he gave her and said cheerfully, "Brother, God said marry two women or three women. I know the well and its cover like the back of my hand. The mother of your children is finished—not an ounce of suppleness or beauty left in her." Noha's mother's migraines grew worse, and Noha started to tell Hend all kinds of stories about her newborn siblings. One day, Noha's father said to her, "I'll kill you if you ever play hopscotch again. Do you want to bring scandal down on us, girl?" So Noha began collecting shards of pottery for her new game.

Hopscotch—that perilous, obscene game—was replaced by the game of beads. Noha takes Hend by the hand and runs off to the pottery workshop behind the Hill Estate. Inside the workshop there were mounds of raw clay and finished crockery and round, smooth, long-necked water jars in red and white, turned on an iron lathe to produce the perfect, narrow holes that neatly disbursed their liquid into the drinker's mouth. The pitchers, unlike the water jars, had large, projecting spouts that shamelessly disgorged their water onto the bare thighs of people washing out in the open. There were other things for sale in the workshop: oven paddles; huge storage jars for water, standing there erect and virile; puffed-up clay jars like pregnant bellies; dovecotes for pigeon chicks to sleep in. The way of the world: forms whimsically created by the master craftsman, then burned in the fiery kiln and laid out on the straw facing the workshop for the passing women to pick up and examine, and perhaps even buy.

Hend and Noha run off together and climb Pharaoh's Hills. In order to reach the pottery workshop they have to cross the open space where the Friday market is held and pass the gypsy camp. They tirelessly collect bits of broken pottery and run back home with their booty. They sit on the doorstep of Amm Mahmud's shop and proceed to round the broken shards into smooth beads that they scoop up and toss with long, experienced fingers as their plastic bracelets jingle merrily on their wrists. But once again Noha's angry mother comes out to drag her daughter away by the hair and pinch her thighs because "the girl has gotten into the habit of wandering around like a stray cat." And that was the last time Hend and Noha ever played together.

She spied on Amm Mahmud's shop in the hope that she would catch a glimpse of her friend making paper cones for the sugar or polishing the slippery floor. Now she only ever saw her sitting behind the iron gate and playing beads alone, every movement executed with a grace and skill that only Noha could possess—the grace and skill of someone who was used to playing alone. When Hend asked about her friend, Noha's mother said: "That's it, no more schooling for her." But that didn't stop Hend from hanging around the iron gate that no one ever opened for her. Her old friend talked to her from the other side with the calmness and self-possession of a little woman. The sculptor of girls visited her before any of the other girls. Her face grew fuller and her body lither, and she walked now with a deliberate, self-conscious stride. Hend watched her behind the gate as she played alone, surrounded by the odor of kerosene coming from the corrugated iron barrels and by plastic containers of oil and canvas sacks of sugar. Noha never came out, and a few months later she disappeared entirely while Fatma al-Qarumiya came and went through the iron gate with her kit of pastes and oils and medicines for nausea and pregnancy, and when Hend asked her about Noha, Fatma laughed that deep, masculine laugh of hers that terrified children and excited the lust of passing men, and said, "The sculptor of girls kidnapped her."

Hend's other friend Hanan was round and heavy with skin the color of wheat, a miniature version of her mother, the lady Umm Hanan the seamstress. Once Noha had gone to live with the sculptor of girls, Hanan and Hend would sit next to each other on the sofa of her mother's house and Hanan would show her the colorful snippets of leftover fabric that she hid in her pockets and used to make blackboard erasers or soft cotton rags for wiping the chalk off your fingers. Hanan was always wiping the board clean and the whole classroom would stare at her round, plump rear end as she did it. Hanan didn't know how to play hopscotch, or beads either. But she was very good at making rag dolls and blackboard wipes. She was also good at cutting out patterns for doll dresses, especially ones with lots of frills—all from the leftover fabric that she gathered from under her mother's sewing machine. She embroidered the dresses with sequins and colored stones and sold them to the girls in the other classes for five milliemes apiece. She drew eyebrows and mouths on her rag dolls with colored pens and sewed two green stones in for eyes. In arts and crafts class she crocheted tablecloths with the duck stitch like a practiced housewife. She also sold crocheted hats that she made herself, as well as scarves and embroidered handkerchiefs. Her passion for embroidery and her quiet perseverance were extraordinary, and she became an expert at making exquisite tablecloths that she called "sunflowers" because they were the color of open sunflowers in all their glorious shades from dark brown to bright sunshine yellow.

The only game that Hanan was good at was 'little house.' She would come to Hend's house and collect the empty matchboxes from the garbage as well as old bottles and cartons. Together they traced out the borders of their imaginary house in the sand with pebbles and scraps and some tree branches and leaves. Everything was now ready to play-act mother and daughter. Hanan was the daughter and called Hend 'mama' or sometimes she was the maid and called her 'ma'am.' She was anything Hend wanted her to be, because Hanan had been trained to obedience. She was sedate and well-behaved, an immovable object, while Hend ran around like a lunatic in the courtyard that hosted an imaginary house of dust full of imaginary stoves and refrigerators and beds.

Sometimes Hend's mother sent her to Umm Hanan's house with clothes that needed altering. Hanan's mother took them in or let them out or shortened them, from one child to the next. Hend skipped happily through the narrow streets covered in straw. Women sat at their doorsteps, washing the dishes and drinking tea or exchanging good-natured insults. Hend liked Umm Hanan's house because it was always full of women, the door always stood wide open, and the hubbub of the sewing machine and the transistor radio gave it a festive atmosphere quite different from that of her own home. Umm Hanan was stout and dark-skinned. Her voice was mellow and pleasant to the ear and she liked to sing. They called her Fathiya Ahmad—after the actress—because she had thin eyebrows that she painted with kohl. Her eyes were deep black, she wore her hair in a chignon perched coquettishly at the side of her head, and she always matched the color of her hat to her outfit. Her voice sent shivers down Hend's spine, especially when she bent over her machine and sang that particular song: "If Only We Could Be Together Again." She also sang songs to make the girls laugh. She wiggled her eyebrows wickedly as she sang: *Pull the curtain against the breeze before the neighbors break our hearts.*

Umm Hanan's breasts were full under the frill of her plunging neckline, but there was still enough room for the scissors and the sewing needle and other little items like her tweezers and eyebrow pencil and change purse. Her round breasts could still be compared to all the usual fruits because she never breastfed any of her three daughters, but gave them to her sister to nurse instead. When she bent over her sewing machine her breasts spilled out over the frills of her dress.

Her house was full of young girls who had come to learn the trade. They called her "ma'am" and Hend never saw them sitting at the machine. Mostly they swept and cooked and scattered water in the street in front of the house to tamp down the dust, but when Umm Hanan began to cut out a piece of fabric they huddled around her on the rush mat and tried to memorize her every move. Umm Hanan's mother lived with her. She was an extremely thin old lady with lots of wrinkles. She liked to sit in the sun because it soothed her inflamed eyes, crusted and shut fast with ophthalmia. She quietly peeled the garlic or shelled the peas, only breaking her silence to do her ablutions and pray for the Prophet or tell a few stories to the girls now and then. They had to repeat everything they said to her because she was hard of hearing. Hend knew that she used to bake bread in people's houses like Grandmother Zaynab, but then she retired when the pain in her eyes got worse because of the heat and smoke of the ovens. One day Hend came by with a message. "Mama says can you make some pies for her for Ramadan, grandmother?" Umm Hanan got up in a huff from her spot at the sewing-machine, "Tell mama that we don't work for the Bedouins any more," she said emphatically as she wiggled her eyebrows, "and my mother doesn't make pies or bread any more either." Hend remembers feeling mortified. She didn't understand who these "Bedouins" were in the first place or what her family had to do with them.

Umm Hanan played with the radio dial every few hours to find her favorite songs. At some point, she started to refuse the mending work that Hend brought from her mother. "Tell your mother that I don't do alterations any more," she said bluntly. "My scissors only cut brand new clothes now." Hend stared at the floor self-consciously as she stood there with the old clothes in her hand. Umm Hanan must have felt sorry for her because she took them gently and said, "All right then, just this once for mama's sake. But tell her that my scissors are legendary and that she'll never see anything like the cut of my sleeves." Hend nodded her head obediently and went to sit next to the old grandmother, who told her the story of 'Hend the daughter of King Nu'man.' She watched the girls as they scrubbed the pots and pans. They stole glances at Umm Hanan as she yawned and said, "My back is killing me, girls. One of you can fix this piece." She left the machine to them and stretched out on her stomach on the rush mat. She nodded off as one of the girls massaged her back. Sometimes they plucked stray hairs from her eyebrows or her plump legs without being asked, as if they'd been trained from the start to do that kind of thing. Umm Hanan emerged from these sessions glowing and smooth-skinned, looking just like Fathiya Ahmad, especially when the kohl smudged in circles under her eyes. Her men-friends were in the habit of dropping by the house. They walked in as though they owned the place, stretching out comfortably in the living room with its three clean, brightly colored sofas. Umm Hanan's door was never shut fast, and anyone outside could easily hear her echoing laugh and the sound of her fine, plaintive voice as she sang.

Hanan pulls Hend by the hand up to the roof. They climb the wooden ladder and lie down together on the straw. Hanan weeps, and her voice sounds exactly like her mother's. "She wants to get married. Every day she tells me the same thing. 'I don't know where your father is. From the day he left for Jordan he hasn't sent a word or a penny. He said he'd be back in the blink of an eye but he never came. I'm not going to stay single like this forever, living without a man, and you're older now and you've got to understand.'"

Hanan's mother didn't get married after all, but certainly not for lack of suitors. Hanan grew up and sprouted full breasts and rounded buttocks before any of the other girls. This provoked the Arabic teacher and he would make her wipe the blackboard on purpose so that he could examine the telltale signs of her approaching womanhood at his leisure. He talked a lot about the ancient Bedouins' passion for female posteriors. Hanan disappeared from class suddenly, like Noha, and when Hend took a bag of oranges and went to visit her, ill with a stomachache at home, Umm Hanan laughed coquettishly and purred, "That's it . . . your little friend is a woman now." Hend sat next to Hanan and Hanan told her about the talcum powder and her aching legs and the cramps. Hend thought long and hard about the sculptor of girls and wondered why he still hadn't paid her a visit, she alone among all the girls. She waited impatiently for him to come and take her as far away as possible.

Soon, different kinds of guests started to come to Umm Hanan's house. Some of them wore the white Bedouin headdress. They looked a lot like Hend's uncles, impassive under the weight of their heavy robes. A few months later, one of them carried Hanan off to his distant country, a place even further away than the Red Estate, or Jordan, or anyplace Hend had ever heard of. Umm Hanan abandoned her sewing machine and built two new rooms out of red brick. She began to shut her door fast from then on, a new door made of elaborately carved wood. The townswomen would come to examine her merchandise: Saudi gowns and Gulf-style scarves, black veils and heavy stockings for covered women. She changed her title from "the lady" Umm Hanan to "the hajja" Umm Hanan. She took to visiting the blessed city of Medina and the Prophet's tomb every few months and she'd come back carrying suitcases full of merchandise. She would sell and bargain and swear on the blessed Prophet's tomb that she had "loved" it (meaning that she had kissed it) with her own two lips. She insisted that she never made any profit, and that she only did it for the love of God. She also began to praise the virtue of the town's young women to the skies and she offered to marry them off in those pure and blessed faraway countries, free of charge, her only recompense being the

99

approval of the Creator of all things, and the joy of settling the girls—especially the youngest of them—comfortably in life. The neighbors started to place all their hopes in her and her business. They sent the spinsters to work as servants and married off the youngest and prettiest of their daughters in distant Saudi Arabia. They began to say that her visits were blessed, especially when she knocked on their doors in her elaborately embroidered velvet gown and repeated any one of her newly acquired expressions: "May God reward you with good" and "May God permit me to do a good deed with every step" and "in God's keeping"—those turns of phrase that clothed her in an aura of strength and purpose.

Hend sat alone in her classroom at the Muqawi School. She was the only girl left in the class now that all the other girls had disappeared, one after the other. She sat there, quiet and well-behaved, convinced that hopscotch was a shameful game that made girls spread their legs and that beads were sinful because they disturbed the peace of households and brought about their ruin. She even began to hate 'little house' because houses were places that thrived on wretchedness and calamity. After Hanan disappeared, she didn't want to have friends any more, or maybe she just didn't know how to make them. She started to refer to the people she met as 'classmates' or 'acquaintances.'

Here in Brooklyn, she waits for the phone to ring or for a strange woman to smile at her on the street. She doesn't see Fatima any more either. "Everybody in this city is running around after something. Everybody is busy," she would say to make herself feel better. She walks alone toward Atlantic Avenue. The winter rain falls steadily and the homeless people hide in the subway station or make a quick dash for the Dunkin' Donuts. They sit alone and glance longingly at strangers with whom they hope to exchange a smile or a few simple words. The rain falls on the glass windows of the coffeeshop and she watches the solitary drops and thinks how closely she fits in with the wretchedness around her. As she walks down the long avenue she passes the halal butchers, the Islamic

Center, and the stores that sell fragrant oils and religious books about the torments of hell, pilgrimage clothes and velvet Meccan prayer rugs and short white Pakistani jalabas and so many different kinds of headscarves. Sometimes she rides the bus from Atlantic Avenue in the north of Brooklyn to Coney Island or Brighton Beach in the south. She sits next to the window and remembers how she used to love watching the world go by from the window of the old Cadillac. She stays on the bus till the end of the line and then rides back again, without getting off.

She sits down on the wooden bench in front of Coco Bar, near his school. The boy she's waiting for has grown taller somehow. He walks a few steps ahead of her in silence. He answers her questions abruptly, *"Fine,"* and then he suddenly says this: "Life is hard here. But you have to keep dreaming because dreams do come true sometimes." She has no idea where he got that from, but she tells him that she likes the way he pronounces the words in English. *"Dreams come true sometimes, Mom."*

Fulton Street

Fulton Street runs through the heart of Brooklyn. A small one-story building with a back garden and terrace stands on a small side street opposite a church. They call it the Refugee Assistance Agency. She goes there every week and takes her place next to the young women, and older ones like herself, who come here looking for work and food stamps or a meager weekly handout. The women are from Burma and Bosnia, Iraqi women in cheerless black robes, fair-skinned Kurdish women, and Afghans with bright, flushed faces.

Hend always sits next to Nazahat. Nazahat, who fled Bosnia years ago, had a habit of producing an ID card from her pocket every so often to prove that she used to be a doctor back home in a city that Hend had never heard of. Her face was small and pink and she wore thick prescription glasses that gave her a dignified look. Her voice was measured and grave—as a doctor's voice should be—and her limited English was Russian-accented. Thanks to her many skills, Nazahat was much sought after by immigrants with no health insurance from the communities scattered on the peripheries of Brooklyn and particularly in Canarsie. The Refugee Assistance Agency was full of them: legal and illegal immigrants, many from conservative Yemeni Muslim families who all lived together in big houses. Nazahat's skills opened the door to their world. She was an expert at diagnosing and treating all kinds of aches and pains.

She took her patients' pulse and checked their blood pressure and temperature. She examined pregnant and nursing women, and the families always sent for her in emergencies. They called her "doctor" and they trusted her because she was a Muslim, and therefore permitted to examine the private parts of other Muslims. She also carried a small portable sewing machine with her wherever she went. She would go from home to home and alter the voluminous black abayas at the waist or neckline or hips—shapeless clothing that was transported to New York by merchants and returning pilgrims in standard sizes.

Nazahat's hands were accomplished hands, small and agile and crisscrossed with minute veins, the hands of a miracle worker. The only Arabic words she understood were "God willing," "thank God," "take it out here," "take it in there," and a few other basic expressions that she needed to communicate with her clients— especially with the old matriarch who ran all those households from her permanent spot on the prayer rug where she constantly murmured to her beads, "There is no power or mercy save in God." The young ones didn't resemble their mothers at all. They wore designer clothes and spoke fluent American English in spite of the fact that they usually never made it past junior high school because the grandmother promptly arranged early marriages for them from her spot on the prayer rug. Nazahat's services were especially in demand during the marriage season. She was the one who cut and sewed trousseaux and prepared facials and treated pelvic inflammations and prescribed ointments of various kinds. She played the roles of bathhouse attendant and nurse all wrapped up in one. The matriarch, who chewed on mouthfuls of qat grown in the small garden behind the house and rubbed her hands with saffron and aloe musk, was fond of her, and called her "a true Muslim." Nazahat also did the shopping for her Yemeni clients because they didn't like to send their women to the supermarket. The women mostly took care of the housework and didn't go out at all except in the company of their husbands. Hend discovered that many of these wealthy Yemeni families owned most of the delis in Brooklyn as well as a good number of the Brooklyn Laundry Clean franchise stores, and that they competed with the Mexicans in the construction business. They had started out as small contractors, then expanded into business dynasties, marrying among themselves and forming a 'ghetto' that stretched from Canarsie to Fifth Avenue.

Nazahat sat on her chair in the waiting room of the Refugee Assistance Agency between Hend and a group of young Bosnian women covered from head to foot, and she told Hend about Omar Azzam. She said that he was very rich and very generous with his money and that he supported dozens of Muslim families with monthly stipends. She urged Hend to meet his wife, Erica, an American girl who saw the light and converted to Islam thanks to him, and who was very charitable to the Muslim refugees in Brooklyn. Omar Azzam was rich—richer than anyone could imagine, richer even than his Yemeni partners in the construction and deli business. Hend turned her face to the window to escape the conversation. "That kind of charity isn't for me," she said. "I don't have anything to do with the God that you people are always talking about. Or at least I'm trying to forget Him for now." Nazahat turned her back on Hend and didn't say another word.

The group of women who sat to the side at a distance from the circle of men were plump like her. Their rear ends were heavy and they used obscure body language to reply to simple questions like "How are you?" There was something slightly bizarre about them. Their transparent Uzbek scarves partially concealed their faces, and they wore strange dresses printed with primitive shapes — squares and triangles — in bright colors, red and green like the flags of disappeared nations drowned in some sea. They smiled for no reason. Their children would grow up and learn to speak American English and they would never ask after their absent fathers. Their papers were marked, "physical and emotional abuse . . . humanitarian asylum"—phrases that Hend understood too well. A large group of relatively young men also waited at the agency. Most of them were from Burma and Afghanistan and they exchanged a few list-less words until their turn came to receive their checks. They didn't talk much because each of them was preoccupied with his own affairs. They didn't share their stories like the women did because they wanted to forget them. They looked forward to becoming ordinary American citizens in a few years and never again having to answer the question, "Where do you come from?"

Abdul approached her with a big smile on his face. He was twenty years younger than her and desperate to find a job and a woman to keep him company. She smiled back but she didn't want to get involved in a conversation because he talked too much and wasn't very intelligent. He asked her the same question that he asked everyone, just to pass the time.

"Are you from the agency?"

She shook her head.

"Arab?"

She nodded.

"Iraqi?"

She shook her head.

"Ah. Palestinian, right?"

She shook her head. "I'm Egyptian," she answered curtly, hoping to nip the conversation in the bud.

"Christian, right?"

She didn't reply. She withdrew into herself even more, but Abdul wasn't giving up.

"Do you go to the English class?"

She nodded.

"And the job training classes?"

She shook her head no. Her head was getting tired from all this shaking, but he still wouldn't shut up. He wanted to show off, to prove to her that he was some kind of expert on refugee affairs. He told her that he was from Afghanistan, and she thought how his small brown eyes were like the eyes of a mountain wolf. He volunteered his story, a pack of lies like everyone else's in this place.

They lied to cover up things that they didn't want anyone to know and they buried the truth deep down, deeper than anybody could see. He told her that he used to work for the American army, and he said it proudly.

Abdul went out to the terrace to smoke. She followed him because she wanted to bum a cigarette, to exhale her anxiety along with the smoke, to get away from the crowd. The agency office was part of the library, just a small room looking out onto Park Avenue. The terrace was full of wooden chairs too. He sat on one of them and crossed his legs. The sun glanced off his coal-black hair and lit up his athletic, martial build. He handed her a cigarette as he leaned back in his chair against the railing. She sat on the other side of the terrace and smoked in silence.

Abdul grinned because he had finally found someone to talk to. "Do you pray?"

She shook her head no. She refused words, words were meaningless. Only silent gestures could guarantee an existence free of lies.

"Do you like vodka?" he asked lewdly. Hend thought that he must be mocking her loneliness because he asked the question as though he were making her a generous offer. He said it with the cunning of a restless wolf looking for a partner to howl at the moon with. She laughed because she hadn't expected that he would try to seduce her.

"I like vodka, but I don't go out with children," she replied playfully. Then she looked him straight in the eye and told him that she preferred to drink alone because when she got drunk she always cried a lot and then passed out. She added that men didn't usually like to witness this disappointing little drama. He nodded his head shrewdly this time, evidently convinced of the wisdom of her observation, and returned to a more general line of questioning.

"Are there American military bases in Egypt? Did you ever work at any of them?" She didn't respond to this, and he continued: "I used to translate for the Americans." He laughed and stubbed out his cigarette with his shoe. "I translated for them, I brought them information and hashish and other stuff. We used to drink Russian vodka and smoke the best Afghan hash together." He reached out to touch her hair. "Do you like Afghan hashish?"

She laughed in spite of herself because he was even more of a child than she thought at first. She imagined that he wished he could just burst into tears, that he was terribly homesick because he still hadn't found the paradise that he was desperately looking for. Hend had smoked hash just once in her life, but she didn't tell him this. She only did it because all she wanted to do was write, so much so that she felt she would die if the bitter mountain of words stayed trapped inside her. She had to finish her first and only manuscript, *I Am Like No Other*, but writing is intractable, like a wounded woman, and at some point she realized that, after all was said and done, she was incapable of healing those wounds. She cried all the time and she desperately searched in every corner for that little girl who used to live inside her. She wanted to burrow deep inside the cocoon of her fears, and that's why she tried smoking the pungent, sticky drug just once, so that she could pick up the pen and set it to paper again. But she still couldn't write. She vomited, then she slept for a long time, and when she woke she found that her son, who was still crawling back then, had thrown his tiny body over her face. "Mama, Mamaaa!" he bawled. He was hungry and wet from head to foot and the acrid smell of his urine burned her nostrils.

She didn't tell Abdul any of this because she knew he wouldn't understand. He, meanwhile, was making a superhuman effort to discover the effects of his manly powers on her. "Afghani hash is moist and soft," he whispered suggestively, tracing an arc in the shape of a woman's backside with his hands. She ignored him.

The smell of hashish drifted from Abdul's cigarette and it immediately reminded her of her old Arabic teacher. She used to worship her Arabic teachers for some mysterious reason. Maybe it had something to do with the smell of hashish that clung to their clothes, or their poise and style. They seemed to her to exude a kind of masculine magic. The Arabic teacher was always staring at her friend

Hanan's breasts, exactly at her breasts, two small round lovely pro-
trusions that got bigger by the day. The man was tenacious and
inscrutable and he would often reel off difficult and dazzling tongue
twisters and make Hanan repeat them quickly, just for fun. Hanan
always laughed out loud at the mistakes she made. Her small breasts
would shake in hilarity and this pleased him to no end. The Arabic teacher was a very distinguished man, although everyone knew
that he was the only son of Grandmother Zaynab who insisted she
wasn't a servant even if she worked in people's houses. She did it
because "her hand was blessed when it came to cooking and baking and crushing the wheat or milking the cows." Of course this was
the same hand that had raised a man whose shirts were always clean
and elegant and whose coal-black, fragrant hair was always meticulously groomed. He was—as the whole school knew—a serious and
respectable man, addicted to the cigarettes that Mahmud the grocer
sold and particularly fond of Hanan and her mother the seamstress.
People often saw him coming and going from Umm Hanan's house
and she had been heard serenading him with the popular song "So
What If He's Dark-skinned, It's the Secret of His Beauty." He leaned
on the table at which Hanan and her mother sat and grinned at the
girl. Her plump cheeks flushed pink, a carbon copy of her mother.
He had first noticed this resemblance when his class was suddenly
emptied of girls and he started to miss their intoxicating perfume.
More than once Emile the principal had come into the classroom
to warn him, "You're going to bring catastrophe down on our heads,
man!" But he was too busy observing Hanan's miraculous transfor-
mation from a child into a woman to pay any attention to the worried
schoolmaster. As for Hend, he was mostly interested in her literary
skills. She was now able to read and correct the other students' exer-
cises and write their names on the board and even conduct part of
the lesson as he lounged on his chair at the front of the class and
exchanged innocent pleasantries with his favorite student.

At the same time that Umm Hanan was borrowing talcum powder from the neighbors in an attempt to ascertain the onslaught of

her daughter's early puberty, the Arabic teacher was busy sending Hanan letters warning her that she would be expelled from school if she didn't come back. Neither Hanan nor her mother bothered to read these letters and Hanan stayed put at home. The Arabic teacher, anxious and distracted, was now obliged to focus his attention on Hend, who realized that she would have to face him alone. She explained the rules of grammar and rhetoric to her classmates while he emptied cigarettes with the cartridge of his pen and stuffed them again with hashish. He started to carry a thin cane around and would get angry for no reason and shout insults ("You cattle!") at his students because, as he said, they came to school without cleaning the dung off their plastic shoes and never washed their rough hands, stained green from cutting clover in the fields. Most of Hend's classmates generally considered school to be a kind of rest period or napping time from their heavy work in the fields and they sat in class with stupid expressions on their faces and fought among each other rancorously—which only proved the teacher's point. He took to beating them with his cane. He would stretch them out over his chair and give the backs of their legs a good thrashing. The children would get down off the chair, their mouths set in stony silence, trying to hold back their tears. When he finally got tired of giving out beatings he produced his rolling papers and prepared the tobacco and hash mixture while throwing out casual remarks about how cattle never get tired of a good whipping.

Meanwhile, Hend continued to read the lessons out loud in class. Once, when she said to him, "I'm tired, can't someone else do it?" he yanked her brown school apron and said in that high-pitched voice of his that terrified her, "Who do you think you are? A king's daughter? Go on and run back to your papa's house. The girl thinks she's a princess! You Bedouins can go to hell." Hend ran out of the classroom and Mr. Emile the principal ran after her but she didn't stop. She left the Muqawi Primary School behind and walked past the threshing machine and the agricultural cooperative all the way home. From that day on her stomach began to hurt her every time she saw the

Arabic teacher. He never called on her in class again and she just sat there staring at the wall and waiting patiently for the interminable lesson to end. Then the Arabic teacher began to wear a white cap and pray a lot. He even started taking the boys to the school mosque to pray as a group every Friday. A few months later he took the boat to a faraway country called Yemen. He wasn't the only one. In those days, a lot of teachers packed their bags and went there.

Grandmother Zaynab wept copious tears and said, "Son of a bitch, that son of my womb. Son of a bitch, just like his father. He didn't even say, 'Mother, I'm leaving.' He didn't say goodbye to the mother who slaved over him all his life. Never mind, I hope God goes easy on him and puts the wind in his sails with the sea beneath him and his ships full to the brim." God seemed to have answered Grandmother Zaynab's prayers, just as He seemed to have blessed her hands. The teacher came back from Yemen with a prayer mark on his forehead, a handful of Meccan musk in his pocket, and a pure white jilbab. He began to spend all his time in the Nur Mosque. He preached to the people and led the Friday prayers and called out from the minaret. The congregation would listen intently to his loud voice as he said things like, "O Prophet of God, your people are overrun by wolves," and his words brought tears to their eyes. He became famous for his eloquence and zeal. He opened a store selling plastic household goods, the first of its kind in town. He called it 'al-Baraka.' Then he opened a ceramics and tile shop to cater to the owners of all the new brick houses that were springing up in town. He called it 'al-Quds.' Then he opened a number of franchises specializing in electrical products and called them 'al-Furqan.' Pharaoh's Hills had become a different place by then, and Hend would often grow disoriented as she led her father on their walks from the reception house to the Heights.

Abdul playfully tugged on a strand of her hair, bringing her back to him from the maze of her memories. A feeling of anger and humiliation washed over her. She told him sharply that she didn't like hashish, or children who play at being grownups, or translators and spies—that, in fact, she didn't like anything about him. She told him that she didn't believe in anything any more and that as far as she was concerned, he, Abdul, was nothing but a stupid kid.

Abdul just laughed at this harangue and asked her with the cunning of a mountain wolf: "So you're the ambassadress of good intentions. They're giving you legal residency and food stamps and sympathy for free. Or maybe you're the ghost of Mother Teresa come from the high seas to strike the fear of God into me...."

Abdul's comment hurt her. He didn't understand why she was here—not that she did either. It hurt her because she knew that she was more decent and principled than that. He just didn't understand. She turned her back on him, and he added a parting shot: "And on top of everything you have a big ass, and I don't like women whose rear ends are as big as Mount Sinai."

He laughed at his own joke, pleased to show off his command of American slang and his ability to humiliate people coldly, with a smile and not a trace of anger. She pictured him as a mountain wolf cub raised at the teat of an American commando unit, an expert on vodka and hashish and blasphemy, with nothing better to do than to taunt a solitary and wretched woman like herself.

Pluto in Capricorn

low, persistent, and cautious. Winterish and loves routine. Idealistic and ambitious. Conservative; prepared to scale mountains to attain his goals. Kind, ethical, and noble. A careful and tireless striver, like all Capricorn men who know how to plan each step calmly, with confidence and great patience, but who jealously hide their disappointment in failure. They meet adversity with stubborn and solitary persistence, bouncing back and starting all over again. The description fit him perfectly, her friend who died.

The winter rain pounded the glass windows of the downtown shops as Hend sat next to her friend in the Tak'iba Café. They always went to the same downtown cafés together. Her friend knew all the waiters by name. He exchanged greetings with them, asked them how they were doing and which villages they came from. They sat by the window and watched the rivulets of water streaming down the sidewalks. The glass reflected his tense face as he asked her the same old questions, questions she'd grown tired of:

"How's life?"

"Well, it's over now."

"You've still got a lot ahead of you. You're not going to die."

He reminded her of her son when he said things like that. She replied with the same listless, resigned tone: "Where will I go in the end?"

"I don't know," he frowned. "I wish we all knew where we'll end up. Things would be much easier."

They fell into a gloomy silence and drew long and hard on their water pipes. Again, he picked up the thread of the conversation and asked her about things that she preferred not to talk about.

"And what about him?"

She didn't answer. In fact, she didn't have any news of her husband. No one knew where he had disappeared to, or why. She was tired of people asking her about him. As far as she was concerned, he was just someone who had vanished from her life without a trace.

They avoided each other's eyes and her friend the Capricorn tried to change the subject. She liked wandering the city streets with him because he was easygoing and respected her long silences. As he walked by her side she was suddenly overcome by the feeling that still haunts her now: a feeling of emptiness and futility and a yearning to share her loneliness with another human being. Her Capricorn friend could talk endlessly. He told her all kinds of stories about the city's many squares and alleys and buildings. Sometimes he talked just to avoid the subjects that upset her. "This is Bab al-Luq Square. Do you know why they call it that? People from across the city used to meet here. First it was called Bab al-Liqa'—the Meeting Gate—then later Bab al-Luq." She nodded her head for lack of anything to say. He narrated the history of the small, obscure cafés that they passed on their walk: "This is the Sphinx Café. We used to come here after going to see a movie at Cinema Radio. Cinema Radio was something else in those days." A few streets further on, he stops and points. "The Indian Cultural Center is here, in this passageway. The Indian Teahouse is right next door. It used to be one of the loveliest cafés in the city. The intellectual crowd used to come here, but the artists mostly preferred the Rex Café on the corner of Imad al-Din Street."

She had no idea where Imad al-Din Street was. The endless spider web of streets confused her, but she kept nodding her head encouragingly. "Naguib al-Rihani and Stephan Rosti and Anwar

Wagdi used to go to the Rex. All the big film contracts were signed here—right here, on these very tables." He swore to her that he once saw the actor Ahmad Mazhar sitting at the Rex. He was obviously very proud of the fact.

"My friend Yahya used to come here. His dream was to write a screenplay especially for Nadia Lutfi. Do you know what the café was originally?"

"What?"

"A barber shop," he replied, grinning broadly.

He told the same stories every time but she didn't mind because, of all the people she knew, he alone still saw her as she imagined herself to be. To him, she never grew older and more abject with the passing days. He didn't notice the slight stoop she had acquired thanks to the painful stitches under her belly from the operation that followed her miscarriage. To him she didn't appear ashen and overweight and pitiful—quite the contrary. He said that she looked like Zubeida Tharwat, Suad Hosni, and Nancy Agram all rolled into one. His presence was a source of delight to her. He made her feel beautiful in spite of everything. She was in the habit of wearing a black, mannish blazer that she referred to a little sheepishly as "sporty" but she really only wore it to hide things she would rather not think about, like her rear end which kept getting bigger by the day. Her simple 'sporty' clothes screened off her fear of other tell-tale markers of her age, like her absentmindedness, her impatience, her constant fatigue, her numerous delusions, and her enormous need to walk and walk with no particular goal in mind. She tried to explain all this to him but couldn't make him understand.

She smokes her cigarette slowly because she dreads coming to the end of it. She smokes it down to the filter, then stretches out on the bed, and the traces of chalk on her fingers and under her nails fill her with a feeling of exhaustion. Sometimes, she prays at night to ward off her loneliness.

She talked to him enthusiastically about the planets whenever she got bored of the story of the twin lions guarding Qasr al-Nil

Bridge, or Princess Nazli's palace and Imad al-Din Street or the Café of the Dumb. She said to him, "I've cast your horoscope. Congratulations."

"What does it say? Tell me."

"It says that Jupiter is in the House of Capricorn this year. Jupiter is the planet of great fortune. It will be an exceptional year for you, my dear goat. Dust will turn to gold in your hands. All the planets are lined up behind you and every single month of the coming year will bring you good things. New horizons will open up before you, and many promises will be fulfilled. Now is the time to harvest fame and love and to exercise that masterful charm of yours to conquer the hearts of one and all."

He laughed happily. He laughed so hard that his face became an indistinct blur.

"Do you really believe that stuff?"

"Sometimes I need to believe it."

"And you? What does your horoscope say?"

"'My friend the Cancer, you're at rock bottom!'"

"You're always at rock bottom! Always hugging that bag of yours to your chest even when you're sitting down, as if you've got to hurry off for an appointment at any moment. You're always anxious. You never stay in one place for more than a few minutes. Do you know that Yahya never traveled in his whole life? The only time he set foot outside Cairo and went to Alexandria, he got into the accident and died."

"Maybe. Who's Yahya?"

"Yahya, my friend. If he'd met you he would have really liked you."

"Maybe."

"And maybe then you would have stayed here forever and not thought about going away."

"Maybe."

They drew deeply on their water pipes when the silence fell between them and the smoky haze settled around their shared melancholy and wrapped it in a close veil. Then she picked up her bag, which was full of papers and chalk and desolation, and went.

Hend thinks about how she had never owned a suitcase in her whole life, how there were never any suitcases in their house, only huge wooden chests, left over from the days of the caravans that she had heard tell of and that her mother now used for storing grain and other things. "It's in the Nabulsi soap chest," her mother would say with a hint of pride in her voice, or, "It's on top of the trellis chest." The chests grew old and ratty like everything else in their house. Rats scurried around merrily underneath them and the long years of neglect swathed them in an envelope of grease and enigmatic odors.

Her mother never owned a suitcase either. Hend wonders how she made the trip from her father's house to her husband's without any suitcases. It seemed that she had never gone anyplace else before her marriage. Even on those occasions when she got angry and put on her black dress, determined to leave the house forever, it never occurred to her to take anything with her. She would dry her eyes with a handkerchief as the children clung to the hem of her dress ("Mama, take me with you!"), but her mother never took anyone with her, for the simple reason that she never ended up leaving the house. She would go back into her room and shut the door fast behind her, and Hend's own dreams of escape slowly collapsed under the weight of her mother's muffled sobs.

Her father owned a single small briefcase, but it wasn't made for traveling. It never occurred to him to leave the town bounded by small villages that he had grown up in. The briefcase was full of papers: legal briefs and contracts and petitions that he had been entrusted with and that he took very seriously. He pored over them endlessly. It was a way of showing off how important he was, and also of proving to those who might want to forget it that he held a graduate degree in law. But the truth was that he didn't give a damn about courts or briefs because he believed that everything could be solved by direct negotiation between the parties concerned. He didn't like to leave his house, and the times that Hend traveled with him were few and far between. The white Cadillac crossed the mud flats called Pharaoh's Springs; Shepherd's Hills, where communities of gypsies and nomadic Bedouins lived in canvas tents pitched on the edge of a brackish swamp; the Bedouin Estate, an endless sandy plain bordered by farms and small, isolated villages; the Lady's Estate; the Faridiya Estate; the Hill Estate; and the School Estate. The long green ribbon unwound itself along miscellaneous parcels of land until it emptied into the road that led to the gates of Cairo, that faraway city that people simply called 'Egypt.'

They entered the city from the east and the neighborhood of Heliopolis where most of her uncles lived (Hend no longer remembers those long-ago visits that she paid them as a child). They always made the same stops: the pastry shop Gatineau, Omar Effendi, the fancy medical complex where they went for doctors' visits and lab results. They would while away the hour before one of these appointments at Groppi, the famous confectioner in Tal'at Harb Square. Her father would slowly sip his coffee as her mother finished up her window-shopping on nearby Qasr al-Nil Street. Her father loved to recount the origins of the names of the busy streets they walked down, especially the ones named after famous leaders of the nationalist movement, but in spite of his encyclopedic knowledge he somehow always managed to get lost. He would stop at the corner of Muhammad Mahmud Pasha Street, the leader of the Free Constitutionalists Party, and say, "He was a great man." Her mother nodded her head knowingly as she tottered behind him in her high-heeled shoes. "And this, my dear, is Sherif Pasha Street. Sherif Pasha oversaw the drafting of Egypt's first constitution and he was responsible for outlawing the slave trade." Her mother sighed. She was thinking about things that were much more important than the history of Egyptian liberalism, things like doctors' appointments and lab results and glass show-windows. She held Hend's wrist in a viselike grip to keep her from running off and getting lost in the crowded, dangerous squares that were full of itinerant peddlers. The three of them stumbled around the maze of streets with a growing sense of claustrophobia. Her frustrated mother declared that the popular saying, "The person who built Cairo must have been a confectioner," was sheer nonsense and that God had thankfully spared them the hell of having to live in this city.

They took the road back home in a hurry because the days were short and it got dark early. On the return journey, her mother carried her on her lap. Her plump, soft legs were sheathed in velvety stockings and she wore a typical regional dress printed with big flowers and a blue coat lined with satin. They always went back the same night because her father was only comfortable sleeping in his own bed and because her mother had left half a dozen small kids behind and because driving at night was much more comfortable than driving by day. At night she missed the blue of the sky and her dreams of flight were thrown into sharper relief: "Papa, I want to be an airline stewardess."

"Over my dead body!" He laughed. "No daughter of mine is going to wait on people." She didn't understand what he meant by "wait on people." All she knew was that airplanes fly high up in the sky, and she could already picture herself as an elegant stewardess pulling a suitcase and a pile of dreams behind her. She fell silent for a while, then piped up again. "Papa, I want to grow up and be an astrophysicist." This time her mother answered wryly. "You just want to fly off into space and leave us behind, don't you?" The cold wind came in through the window. She fell asleep on the way, and didn't see the small farms wrapped in the silence of the dark night.

Hend remembers now that the only time her father went on a long trip was to Mecca for the pilgrimage. But he didn't stay long. He came back well before any of the other pilgrims—who inevitably fell in love with the noble lands of the Prophet—and he excused this shortcoming by declaring it to be "an unlivable place. No wonder the Prophet emigrated!" Her mother interpreted this declaration as a manifestation of his eternal idleness. To her lasting chagrin, her husband had no desire to seek his fortune in the wealthy Gulf countries like everyone else. All he did was act strangely and endlessly hang around in reception houses, his own and other people's, always trying to solve problems that were no business of his. She was always complaining that he would never fix the universe, just fritter away his money—hers and her children's. But she was afraid to tell him what was in her heart, and he refused to listen anyway. She would only sigh and dab at her tears and watch him from a distance as he sat every evening on the portico of the reception house on the hill and lit the fire and invited any and all who passed by on the path to come in for some tea. "Please make yourself at home . . . you're welcome, by God. . . ." Even after all his friends packed their suitcases and went off to find jobs in the oilfields, her mother still hoped that he could be persuaded to go too. Meanwhile she overheard him declaring his firm intention to stay put to Doctor Shamil the pharmacist (who eventually decided to emigrate to Libya): "Oh no, Shamil, I'm neither poor nor hungry—the hell with oil contracts! I've got a house of my own and my father's land from al-Sheikh to Ard al-Haysh. You go and good luck to you, but me—never."

And so the father stayed behind and tended the fire in front of the reception house and Hend would sit next to him and say, "Papa, I want to travel." He told her that life was one big journey, and that she would certainly travel a lot, maybe even get altogether sick of traveling when she grew up. "Papa will be a lonely old man by then and no one will want to keep him company any more." He predicted that, by that time, he would no longer be able to see her when she stood before him because he would be blind, and would have to rely on his sense of smell to know his own daughter, his beloved daughter. Who knows? he would say, maybe her presence would even restore his sight, just like in the story of the Prophet Jacob, and then she would become a cane for him to lean on in his old age, and he would take her by the hand and they would walk together from way up on the hill down to the gypsy camps. These prophecies always made Hend laugh. Satisfied, her father would then move on to the story of the Prophet Joseph.

Hend gazed at their house and it looked old and squat and decrepit to her because of the new, multistoried buildings of red brick burned in kilns that had sprung up all over the surrounding marshland. Its old wooden roof could no longer support the stagnant rainwater that gathered in pools on cold winter days. Her mother hurried to put a tray with clay jars and a few brass pots under the holes in the roof in the living room. She could hear the drops of water falling rhythmically into the receptacles at night, and the fire in the stove did nothing to warm the room teeming with sleeping children. Her father came home late and she heard his slow steps approaching the door. He stopped in sometimes to check on the sleeping children wrapped in blankets that had grown worn and threadbare, and he sighed and rubbed his hands anxiously. In the morning he sat in the living room surrounded by his romping children and felt vindicated. "Who would leave all these blessings behind for a bit of money?" he murmured to himself.

The "blessings" gradually became bigger and their needs multiplied. The father made a few more signs advertising his expertise at the High Court of Appeals and distributed them in the center of villages farther afield. He took to calling the reception house his "office" but he still wouldn't go abroad, even after the whole village had gone. The people he knew dispersed—some of them to Iraq, others to the Gulf—and soon, all kinds of imported velveteen blankets, soft and warm, could be seen hanging on the rooftop clotheslines, and stereo systems from Libya or TV sets from Port Said began to pop up everywhere. He would only smile at all these transformations—the suitcases that came and went to distant places—and shut himself up in his room with the following words on his lips: "Whatever the Levantine wind brings, the Yemeni wind takes away."

Maybe the mysterious phrase was meant for his wife, who had begun to cast an anxious eye on the tattered blankets, and the clothes that she kept patching up time after time for the children who were growing at breakneck speed. But she only nodded her head and held her tongue. Her father slipped his Maria Callas

121

record back into the sleeve covered in writing that no one understood and settled down to smoke and read his book, *Liberalism and Egyptian Modernity*. He was careful that everything should remain just so: stable, distinguished, and tranquil, like the dreams that were growing before his eyes in the shape of his children. He never seemed to have any regrets, even after all the town's houses had emptied of their inhabitants, houses through which gigantic suitcases strapped in ropes came and went with the following words scrawled on them in broad letters: "This bag belongs to Sayyid Abu Ibrahim who lives on the western bank in Mansha" or "This suitcase is from the sons of Antar to their mother who lives on the White Estate." And along with the traffic of traveling suitcases, the entire rhythm of life changed. Fatma al-Qarumiya no longer discreetly carried around her cloth bundle stuffed with odds and ends of women's clothing for sale. She began walking around town with a huge vinyl suitcase on her head that she would open on any random corner and call out, "Port Said satin! Imported nylon and silk! Blooming colors for lovely young girls! Abayas from the Hijaz, and the Prophet's musk!" And while the street across from their house was buzzing with the trade in imported goods, her mother continued to alter their old clothes to fit the next child down the line.

Hend wished she had a dainty red case of her own to take on the long trip that she was sure to make one day. This was why she eagerly appropriated the white handbag that she found sitting in her mother's closet. Her mother let her have it because she never went out anyway, and had no use for it any more. The bag was rectangular and had sharp edges, like the purses that hung on the arms of leading ladies in old movies. Hend put a comb and a mirror in it, as well as a few small bits of paper on which she'd written signed letters to herself, since everybody was writing letters to their absent relatives in those days. But hers were cold and lifeless and they moldered away, unread, in the white handbag.

Hend liked to talk about her father to her friend the Capricorn. He had grown into her closest friend, and the spirals of fretful smoke that he blew out through his mouth reminded her of her father. He reminded her of the old rush mats and the story of the Prophet Joseph, and his presence filled her with a feeling of warmth and security. He really listened to her when she talked, and she knew that he believed in her. She in turn found pleasure in his endless stories and the long walks they took together—just as she used to do with her father. She would fall into a kind of happy trance as she listened to him tell the same story over and over, in the same monotonous tone and with the same quiet enthusiasm. They met without rhyme or reason—they never actually made an appointment to meet—and she never had to weigh her words in his company, never felt self-conscious or obliged to hide her depression. He made her feel that he had been put on this earth just to make her happy, to dedicate his life to the sole purpose of walking with her along the meandering city streets. "This is the Muhammad Ali Club, and this is the old Opera building. And this, my dear, is Jabalaya Street where young lovers used to embrace in the dark. But they're all gone now. There are no more lovers in Egypt."

He told her that he used to live on Mohandiseen Street with his friend Yahya. It was a quiet street, with hardly any traffic, only a few buildings owned by the Othman Company. He told her that Yahya used to like hanging around in Stella Bar, which was very different back then. Sometimes, when he walked a few steps behind her or hung on her every word, or expressed delight in her company, he reminded her of her son. He often said to her, "If Yahya had met you, he would have fallen in love with you, and maybe then you would've been happier."

She didn't know who Yahya was, but the repeated remark made her realize that he understood just how miserable and alone she was. She accepted it as an insight and a form of condolence, though sometimes it struck her as cruel, this yoking of her potential happiness to a dead man that she had never met. She attributed her bad luck to her zodiac. It happens, she thought to herself, that you're born on some summer night and suddenly find that you've been taken hostage by a star: always moving in the wrong direction, always pretending to be strong when in reality you quake in mortal fear, always wanting things but never reaching out for them, never knowing the difference between truth and illusion. It happens that a tentative, murky moon rises, a shape-shifting moon that slowly moves across the dome of the heavens, and your disposition grows dark and changeful like a chameleon. You cry and laugh at the same time, you love and hate at the same time. It happens that milk still seeps from her breasts because her brain has not sent the right signals to her glands. Milky clots cling to the inward-turned nipples, wells of hunger in which her star fate dwells, fast propagating and growing perhaps into small tumors like the ones that killed her mother. Would she die suddenly like her mother, she wonders?

The patterns traced by the stars gave some measure of meaning to her life. She believed that the past and the future formed a cosmic circle whose traces were inscribed on her forehead. She was possessed by the cruel certainty that providence and fate governed the world, and that men and women were powerless to change their destinies, as her mother had believed before her. Hend pictures her mother as she looked in her wedding photo, young and beautiful. They carried her off one day, when night had fallen over that fertile green land, and the old Cadillac spirited her across peaceful deserts and wretched villages plunged in silence. It was summertime and the frogs croaked ferociously from their hiding places in the waterwheels. The car stopped on the long driveway along which electric lamps and colored lanterns had been hung. Their steady hum scattered the thronging mosquitoes as the woman who would become her mother began to explore the old house that was now her home. In the morning, she will inspect the new clothes hanging in her closets. She'll put on the rose-colored dress that reveals the fullness of her breasts and arms, and the rich ornaments that mark her noble ancestry—a necklace of real diamonds and a few gold bracelets in the form of snakes. A few years later she will sell them all to make ends meet.

The old house with the wooden roof was not as lovely as the new bride had imagined it to be, even after she hung her colorful curtains on the windows and a few paintings on the walls. Over the bed and the pillows that would soon grow wet with her tears she hung a painting of a naked and reclining houri of Paradise. She hung a needlepoint canvas depicting a bowl of fruit overflowing with clusters of grapes behind the huge dining table, and another of a tearful child in the bedroom destined for the children to come. The perfume of a mango tree wafted in from behind the balcony as she dusted the cakes with sugar and set out the elegant cane chairs to make the new house worthy of her. Grandmother Zaynab sprinkled the marriage incense in every corner and the guests who had come to pay their respects gossiped about the young bride's hair, done up in small ringlets that delicately framed the edges of her face. Hend imagines that her mother must have been happy at first because she could turn on the radio and listen to all the songs that used to be forbidden to her: "Don't Kiss Me on the Eye, Eye-kisses Divide Lovers."

Her father's house was not far off but people frowned upon a young bride visiting her family, especially in the first years of marriage. They considered it to be a sign of the frivolity and rashness that ruin homes. In any case, Hend's mother could not remember her childhood fondly. Her father, who was also a Bedouin sheikh, married three women and sired many sons and daughters very close to each other in age. He insisted on sending his daughters to a convent school for a few years—as was the custom among the big families in the countryside in those days—so that they would learn to be obedient housewives. Her mother points out a few of her friends in an old photo. "This is the daughter of the mayor of Kafr al-Zayyat. And this is the daughter of the Bedouin chieftain al-Henadi Abd al-Hamid Bek Sultan. And this is the daughter of the mayor Lamlum Basil, my father's paternal cousin." She didn't remember much about her school days except for a few mysterious phrases in French that she had memorized: *Comment ça va? Très bien, bon.* Her mother only used these phrases in exceptional circumstances and when she wanted to show off her education—in conversations with doctors, or strangers who came to visit, for example. She also liked to impress people with her exceptional talent for homemaking, which she gleaned from articles in ladies' magazines that she carefully copied into a notebook in which she kept her recipes for jam and preserves and vegetable casseroles and delicate flaky pastries. With the passing of time, and when the only talent required became how to feed seven mouths on a limited budget, these talents would become the object of general mockery.

After a number of years of useless schooling—as Hend's grandfather saw it—the girls were given lessons at home by Madame Teresa, the seamstress who made their trousseaux: wedding dresses, honeymoon dresses, pregnancy dresses. Madame Teresa carried swatches of fabric around in her pocket and the girls would watch the rapid movement of her scissors in breathless silence as they cut out complicated double cloche and croisé patterns. The clothes were stowed away in boxes, along with the bars of soap and the perfumes and the velvety bedspreads and china and brass sets from Gattegno and Cicurel and Sednaoui, and then they were carried off to the sound of jubilant ululations and the slaughtering of animals. The grandfather did his best to treat all his daughters equally as they set off to meet their destinies, and yet he was fond of insisting that "bringing girls into the world is a calamity that blackens the face and ruins the pocket."

When it was Hend's mother's turn to make her grand exit from her father's house, she was more happily disposed than the other girls. The paternal cousin whom she had the good fortune to be marrying was clean-shaven and handsome, with a spotless white shirt. One of the servant girls had told her that he looked like Yusuf Bey Wahbi. He was a law student at Alexandria University, which meant that she would have to take extra care darning his socks and starching his shirt collars and ironing and scenting his handkerchiefs; she also spent a good deal of time embroidering his dressing gowns to befit his new status as a respectably married man.

The screams of the firstborn filled the house and the labor pains repeated themselves from one swollen belly to the next. The delighted grandfather, puffed up with pride, patted his grandsons on the back, slipped a few banknotes into his daughter's hand, ordered the animals to be slaughtered, then went back home. Five children later, Hend came into the world in the shape of a dark red crab, tormented by its ruling zodiac and its ascendant stars. The father smiled, and the mother murmured apologetically, "Girls are sweet, though." The grandfather didn't come this time, and no animals were slaughtered. By the time Hend was born, her mother had grown much thinner and worn out from raising all those boys, from the constant din they made, from many a sleepless night. There were no more pregnancies after Hend, but her face was always pale and exhausted, as though she had just come back from a grueling journey.

As soon as the mangoes ripened in the summer, the mother would gather her six children into the old Cadillac and go forth on the "journey of winter and summer," as the father sarcastically referred to it. The mother sat next to him and Hend sat in the back seat dreaming of faraway places that she had only ever heard of in stories, mysterious cities with brass domes wreathed in milky white clouds. Every year Hend eagerly waited for the moment when her mother would dab some perfume on her clothes, dust off the black cloak that she wore whenever she left the house, and pack up the jars of marmalade, the tins of homemade biscuits, and the freshly ground coffee that filled the kitchen with its delectable smell.

Hend tugs furiously at her mother's clothes: "Take me with you!" The grandfather's house isn't far, just on the other side of a few empty enclosures and a couple of estates made up of cultivated and fallow land. The car rocks as the wheels pitch into the black mud. The gate of the grandfather's house creaks open slowly and the car passes through. The balcony, plunged in darkness and spread with colorful rugs, waits to receive them as they pile out of the car. Her mother smiles happily as she takes in the sight of the kerosene lanterns hanging gaily in the orange orchards. She embraces her waiting sisters who have also come from their husbands' houses, and they cling to each other in a protracted bout of mirth. Hend watches and listens. The grandfather comes out of his room and puts out his hand to receive the shy, confused kisses of his progeny. The children cling to their mothers' dresses so that the grandfather can identify who they belong to. He never caresses their hair or pats their heads; he only puts out his hand to be kissed. On these trips, the world smelled of mangoes and vibrated with the buzzing of mosquitoes and the croaking of frogs glorying in the brackish waters of summer. The winter trip was shorter. The house echoed with the rustle of sluggish, lazy movement and the close rooms smelled of wood fires and Meccan incense. Even the games they played in winter were calibrated to the rhythms of the long, dark nights. The tales told were longer too, and more enchanting, and Hend would listen in wonder as she wandered feverishly through the corners of her unruly imagination. She dreams of an old Cadillac, its windows open to the breeze, racing across unfamiliar lands and down endless streets, passing villages and dovecotes and mud houses, Bedouin tents and Pharaoh's Hills, and she falls asleep to the whistle of its wheels.

She sleeps and wakes to find that she has grown a few centimeters taller, and that her face in the mirror has acquired a new fullness. Her mother extricates her from the folds of her black cloak and pushes her away. Hend weeps in despair at no longer being allowed to play with her male cousins or scramble up the mango trees with bare legs. They tell her that her loud squeals of delight at being caught in a game of hide and seek are scandalous, and from then on she has to sit next to the Guest, picking at mounds of cotton and twining wicks for the kerosene lamps, long slender wicks on which she hangs her yearning to see the exotic places she hears about in stories.

The years passed and her mother grew more and more exhausted. Her aunts were busier than ever with their own affairs, and the journeys of winter and summer came to an abrupt end: anyway, a woman's place was in her husband's house. Her mother sat in the western balcony and stared out into space while Hend wandered the dusty streets and alleys of the town and prowled around the gypsy camp nearby. Now, whenever she got angry she would say to her mother, "I'm leaving. I'm leaving you all behind for good," and run off to the gypsies. She cried herself to sleep on the straw-covered floor of their huts. She played 'little house' with the gypsy girls and laughed and romped in the straw. Then one day three pairs of arms snatched her up and took her away. Her brothers had worn themselves out looking for her all over town. When they finally brought her back home, her mother pounced on her and pinched her hard in the thigh. The pinch left a blood-red mark to remind her of the warning: "No daughter of mine dares run away from her father's house." So Hend only threatened to run away from then on. She would pack up her clothes in a cloth bundle like the ones the gypsy girls carried around and lay her tear-stained face down to sleep on it. "I'm going," she whispers to herself, "this isn't my home. No one here loves me." Her mother laughs and calls her a little sulker. "All day long, acting like the gypsy girls and the servants," she complained, "and if anyone so much as opens their mouth she packs her clothes and mopes around the house."

On a pitch-black night in a small village in the farthest corner of the Delta, the frogs, reveling in the long summer night, raise a ruckus in the pools of stagnant water and a little red gecko scurries along the wall of an old house. Mosquitoes come in through the open windows. The mother, oppressed by the heat and her eternal solitude, leans her aching back against the wall as the red gecko unfurls its tongue to snap up a mosquito. Hend grew to pity her mother's shattered dreams. She liked to talk to her friend the Capricorn about her mother, about the family's winter trip and summer trip, and she knew that he liked to listen to her. He watched her face tenderly and compassionately as she talked.

"I want to leave here now," she said.

He responded with that steady, composed tone that drove her mad. "You think leaving will make anything better?"

"Maybe I'll have better luck someplace else."

He shook his head as he drew on his water pipe, silently releasing the smoke through his nostrils in one long cloud. The expression on his face puzzled her. He broke the silence with the same old question:

"Have you written anything lately?"

She shook her head in the negative. "I can't seem to."

"Write about the winter trip and the summer trip."

She laughed. She loved him because he believed in her, but her answer was always the same. "Not now."

"You remind me of Yahya."

"Who's Yahya?"

"He was moody like you. I remember when he was in love with Nadia Lutfi."

"What was he like?"

"Like you, moody."

"I never liked Nadia Lutfi."

"If he'd met you, he would have loved you more than Nadia Lutfi."

"So what? How would that have changed anything?"

"Maybe you would've found what you've been looking for. And you wouldn't think of leaving."

"I'm not leaving. I'm trying, just trying."

"Maybe you would've fallen in love with him."

"Maybe."

"And maybe he would have chosen to stay too. To put off his death for a little while longer."

She left him sitting there. She left Egypt too in a last-ditch attempt to escape everything that reminded her of her failure. She fled his attachment to her and the labyrinth of her own emotions. She crossed over to another continent without a word of farewell. She savored her wretchedness and solitude. Pluto confronts her in stony silence, and Jupiter rests in the house of Capricorn: his house. She left without telling him that blessing and misfortune were defiantly conjoined in his stars; that their planets were fated to remain locked in opposing equilibrium, and that she knew he loved her.

Pluto moves into the house of Capricorn slowly. It will stay there for the next twenty-three years. It rumbles on its elliptical course through the galaxy, destroying worlds and rebuilding them. They call it 'the star of misfortune' because it is full of surprises, ponderous, lumbering, and wasted, like pain. It confronts her, threatening to rob her of all that she knows and loves and craves. She looks out through the window and watches the heavy rain splatter across the glass. Her heart beats faster and her dreams are full of terror of the unknown.

She watches her sleeping child with resignation. She embraces him and kisses his hand. A heavy weight presses down on her heart and the sudden contractions fill her with anxiety. She's afraid that he'll wake up alone and terrified, and search in vain for a body that should be lying next to him: "Mama, where are you?" She's afraid of having to abandon him suddenly as her own mother abandoned her. That night she dreamt that she was kissing her mother and the next morning desperately trying to shake her awake. "Mama, where are you?" Her heart is still racing as she leaves a scrap of paper on the table next to him with a few phone numbers and a message — *Mom will be right back* — and descends the stairs to go to the nearby hospital.

She sits in a long row of chairs waiting her turn. She moves between the oxygen masks and the blood pressure meters and the heart monitors and stares at the long hallway full of doctors. She remembers a similar scene long ago — the same machines and the same medicine and food smells, the same white uniforms and glinting steel scalpels laid out on trolleys — and she is filled with dread. Her mother lay practically naked on a mobile stretcher, the thin wires of the heart monitor poking out of her chest. The little girl shrank away, terrified. They wheeled her through the corridors of the hospital to the observation ward as she complained weakly that her chest hurt.

The doctor asks Hend, "Do you have a family history of heart disease?"

"Yes," she answers listlessly. "My father died when he was forty."

"Do you remember which month?"

"I think it was October or November. It was fall and school was about to start."

"Tell me what happened."

"He was telling me the story of the Prophet Solomon. Then suddenly he put his hand on his left shoulder and his heart stopped."

"Was it at night?"

"Yes, around eight in the evening."

"And your mother?"

"She died of breast cancer. Her breasts were always full of milk. My chest hurts too and the milk won't dry up. I've begun to forget things—a lot of things. Am I getting senile?"

"Is there something bothering you these days?"

"I'm always under a lot of stress, but this is the first time I've felt my heart racing like this. I feel it in my shoulder. I've begun to forget, and I don't want to forget. Do you know Hemingway?"

"Yes."

"Hemingway began to lose his memory too. He couldn't write any more because he was losing his memory. I want to write. Am I going to become like him?"

The doctor laughs. She asks Hend to put on her clothes. "I think you're worrying too much. In any case I'll look at the test results. We'll be in touch if there's anything to be concerned about."

She takes the sedatives and leaves. She walks alone down the dark street. Her heartbeat still hasn't calmed down. She opens the door of the house and finds him still asleep in bed. She tears up the piece of paper that she left for him.

She tries to sleep. She dreams that her mother is caressing her hair. In the dream, she weeps bitterly. Her mother wakes her and says, "Go to your son." She asks herself why God torments mothers with milk that won't stop flowing.

The child gets out of bed and puts his arms around her. "Mom, did you go out yesterday?" He asks her this as though she's sitting in the witness box, in a commanding tone or perhaps an anxious one, as though his whole existence depends on her being there by his side. She answers him firmly.

"I was here."

He rubs the sleep and worry from his eyes, then says, "I dreamt that you went out last night."

"But I was here, darling," she repeats soothingly.

"I dreamt that I woke up and didn't find you."

"I'm right here, my love."

She bursts into stinging tears. She rages against Pluto and death, the robber, and childbirth and her own self. She cries bitter tears, and her heart shudders as though it's about to grind to a halt.

Her son puts his arms around her heaving waist. "Mama, what's the matter?"

"I can't breathe."

He pulls her by the hand and makes her lie down on the bed and relax. She takes one of the sedatives but it only makes her cry more, and she says to him, "I had one friend in the whole world. He was kind and gentle. He was born one day under the sign of Capricorn. He died today."

"Your friend?"

She nods her head. It's the way of the world, always losing something, always living in the hope of discovering a truth that doesn't exist.

Her son hugs her close, as though their roles were reversed, she the child and he the parent. "Don't be sad, my darling Mama. I'm here with you."

She hugs him tight and cries on his shoulder. Suddenly her only son becomes her one true friend.

Prospect Park

Atlantic Avenue meets Flatbush at a spot called Prospect Park or 'The Tranquil Garden.' They say that Prospect Park was designed to be a smaller version of Central Park—the giant park that sits in the center of Manhattan—and that all its saplings came from there. They say that the park was first planted soon after the Brooklyn Bridge was finished. It used to be a hamlet surrounded by Dutch poultry farms, vineyards, and dairy factories; then, after the bridge was built, it became a suburb of Manhattan. Over the years its picturesque Dutch architecture attracted writers and composers and bohemians of all kinds. Real estate agents intent on demonstrating the appeal of Brooklyn are sure to point out to you the house that Arthur Miller lived in: "His young wife Marilyn Monroe lived with him in this very building before she became a star. And this is Henry Miller's house. He's the author of *Tropic of Capricorn*. Paul Auster still lives and works here in Brooklyn, and this is the tree that Betty Smith wrote her famous novel about." And in other places they stick up posters of the John Travolta film *Saturday Night Fever*. And the real-estate agents will remind you of all of them if you're looking for a room suitable to house your dreams.

Hend began to learn the map of Park Slope by heart. It helped that a lot of people she met liked to talk about the history of the neighborhood. Many of them were dreamers constantly on the lookout for that one person who would discover their talent, always poring over their notebooks in some early-morning café and waiting for inspiration to seize them. They always looked as though they were on the point of recreating the universe. At night, they eagerly sought out the stray journalist or editor in urbane establishments like Coco Bar and Exotic Bar and the Tea Lounge. Hend rarely set foot in those places. They were way too expensive and she dreaded the kind of attention that a woman by herself might attract. She hurried past them on her daily route—a route that took her nowhere.

Atlantic Avenue is home to the Islamic Center and a host of Arab-owned stores. Narak the Armenian's shop is on the other side of the avenue, closer to the park. Narak sells chessboards and novelty chess pieces as well as books about the game. He also gives lessons to anyone who wants them. Passersby stop at his place, especially kids on their way to the park, drawn by the whimsical shapes of the chess pieces, some of which have storybook themes like Snow White and the Seven Dwarfs. The smiling Armenian relishes the delight of the children around him. They remind him of his days at the Scientific Renaissance School in Baalbek where he used to teach art before emigrating to America. His patience was legendary. He would sit for hours teaching the kids the basic principles of the game by way of a set of magical mathematical formulas.

When Hend goes for a walk in the evening her son walks a few steps ahead of her, grave-faced and contemplative, in an effort to prove to his mother that he's grown up now and capable of walking by himself. He gets all kinds of crazy ideas, like changing his first name because it isn't "cool" enough. He doesn't like his last name either. He wants to call himself Ben, color his hair blonde, and spike it with gel to make it look like Iron Man's. The pimples that have begun to pop up on his forehead upset him terribly. He calls them "acne" in English and spends inordinate amounts of time fixing his hair so that it hides his forehead. He examines his skin in the mirror and decides he likes it because it's "tan" and his friends envy him. One day he says to her, "How come you don't look for *a decent job*?" The word *decent* confuses her. It takes her a minute to figure out what it means in Arabic—'respectable'—and she bristles with resentment. "Why don't you think about your own future and leave me alone?" she replies sharply. Truth be told, she wished she could find that kind of job. She'd like to be a painter or a writer or even an actress. She still dares to hope that some dreams at least can come true at any age.

When they get to the chess shop she leaves him sitting by himself at the table that Narak points to, and goes to sit across the street, on one of the broad, hospitable, rose-tinted stone stoops that descend down to the pavement from the elegant old brownstones. She watches Naguib al-Khalili as he sits at a table in front of the shop in his gray suit, clutching one of his manuscripts and scribbling furiously. She smiles at him and he smiles back, but she doesn't approach him because she knows that he's always desperate for someone to talk to in Arabic—and then there's no stopping him, the same old monologue that leaves her exhausted: how he came to America from a village near Nablus and opened his store, The Groom's Sweets, in 1955; how he covered the walls in pictures of his old village and how the store became famous for its old-school rose-water sherbet and Nabulsi kunafa stuffed with cheese and its small round honey cakes. Every morning the local Arab workers flocked to The Groom's Sweets to buy the cakes that tasted of home and an obscure longing that they struggled to understand.

After decades of grueling work, Naguib al-Khalili now spent most of his time at his friend Narak's shop. He decided to retire when his nephew arrived, in his turn, in Brooklyn and gradually took over the bakery. His nephew was a tall, thin young man called Ziyad. He always dressed in black from head to toe and wore a Palestinian kufiya around his neck. Ziyad came to America to study filmmaking, but the real world got the better of him and he began to work full time in the bakery with his uncle, ordering the sheets of dried apricot and making the fig pastries stuffed with pistachio exactly according to their original recipes because the customers would have nothing else. They came back again and again for a fleeting taste of their childhood. The Nabulsi kunafa was stuffed with real halloumi cheese and the amount of honey in the baklava was just right. The ladyfingers were delicate and crunchy, the red rose sherbet smelled of mountain flowers, and the bitter orange jam seemed to have been aged in your own grandfather's basement, God rest his soul, whatever his name was. Everything reminded them of the smells and tastes of sweet and distant places and times.

Memory thrives on details—details that al-Khalili safeguarded and preserved, and Ziyad too: flexible, cunning details like the crispiness of a single square of sweet kunafa. Ziyad washes his hands of the day's fatigue and tries not to think about his increasingly unlikely dreams. He watches movies with his uncle in the evening—classics or blockbusters—or they go to the theater or an art gallery. Al-Khalili will laugh and say to Ziyad, "The boy's turned out just like his uncle—an artist by God, my son! What else but the love of art brought us here from our country? Your uncle Narak adored painting and playing the violin, and I used to think I was the Prophet Gibran or Mikhail Nu'ayma and that I would write all the poems that Ibn Zaydan himself, God rest his soul, never managed to write. But exile is a son of a bitch, Ziyad, and in the end it only gives you what you've got coming to you anyway."

Ziyad hangs his head. He tries to understand but all he can think about is the film that he dreams of making: a film about Brooklyn's Arab-American community and the domestic problems that they face. Like his uncle, Ziyad adores T.S. Eliot's *The Wasteland* and Walt Whitman's *Leaves of Grass*. He knows Federico García Lorca's poems about Harlem and the Brooklyn Bridge by heart. He is always busy gathering material for his film and planning the scenes that are supposed to take place on the bridge's pedestrian walkway; always thinking about things like funding and shooting and auditioning actors and actresses. He jots down ideas and observations in a small notebook that he keeps in his pocket as he sits behind the counter in The Groom's Sweets. The bakery is a good place to study the different types of Arab immigrants. He considers it to be the source of his inspiration. Naguib al-Khalili loved to boast about this cultured nephew who filled his life with novelty. Ziyad and his Armenian friend were all he had left in the world.

Both Narak and Naguib used to teach at the Scientific Renaissance Secondary School. Later, they traveled across the world together. They still take pleasure in sitting together and reminiscing about those long-ago days. They remember the crowds of Palestinian refugees spread out on the grass in the meadows of Baalbek and endlessly discussing how they would return to their villages once the war was over. When one of the men said that he didn't think they would be able to go back till at least a year or two after the end of the war (this was in 1948), the others jumped in with long encomiums on the Arab armies that would surely win the war in a matter of days. They were so certain that the war would end quickly that some of them had even fed their chickens and cows as usual just before fleeing their homes. Many years passed while the men fought over their predictions. Naguib al-Khalili grew up and Narak turned into a handsome young man who loved to paint and play the violin. He dreamt of going to Egypt and watching the great Naguib al-Rihani in *The Flirtation of Girls* at Cinema Rivoli on Imad al-Din Street. The two friends went to Egypt together, then decided to travel even further. Narak started looking for passage on a ship to New Jersey where his cousins lived. Naguib was also becoming more and more convinced that the return to his village in the Galilee might take longer than he had hoped and that it would be better to work while he waited. So they boarded a boat together in Cyprus and set sail for the land dreamt of by intrepid explorers.

Narak joined his cousins in the grocery business and Naguib took a job as a baker in the shop that now bears the name The Groom's Sweets. Al-Khalili saved every penny he earned so that he could go back and get married in his village once he had rebuilt his father's house, which would no doubt need a lot of repairs after the war. The war lasted for a long time and Naguib forgot all about marriage and the return. His main concern now was to put aside enough money to cover his father's living expenses back in Baalbek and his sister's too. She had stayed on in the village of Sahmata, adamant that she would never leave her country. Naguib fretted about money and worked like a dog, work that never seemed to end, except when life had finally passed him by, and the dreams he had slaved to realize had evaporated into thin air. People who knew him said that he lived an ascetic life, never changing his dull gray trousers and his red checked shirt except on very rare occasions. He didn't smoke and didn't eat much, nor was he in the habit of indulging in games like dominoes or dice in the Arab cafés. He didn't like hanging around in coffeehouses and usually went to bed early, though once in a while he liked to smoke a water pipe because he believed that it strengthened the memory and cleaned out the intestines. Naguib's voice was always pitched low and he steered clear of the dictionary of curses that revolved around mothers and sisters by lowering his head and keeping to himself. He was never known to laugh out loud and, according to many of his oldest friends, he was still a virgin, having never known a woman, having never known anything but the longing to return.

In the old photos from Baalbek during the war, Narak and Naguib sit side by side in the meadow, Narak holding his violin and Naguib looking young and handsome with his pitch-black eyes and gentle, regular features. His hair is slicked back in a Clark Gable cut and he wears a spotless white shirt open at the collar, a stylish blue jacket tailored at a shop in the La'aziya Building in Beirut slung over his shoulder. The memories faded away one by one as the years passed, and so did the dream of return, the only thing remaining of his identity proclaimed in a sheaf of old papers stamped "Palestinian refugee," place of residence: Baalbek, Lebanon. Now there was no question of going back. Now he complained of life in general, and that America was nothing but a big lie. He had developed endless theories about how New York was like a giant meat grinder, its rusted gears immediately tossed in the garbage. He believed that people were not as free here as Americans liked to claim—money and survival were the axis on which everything turned. "What kind of life is it that forces you to bow down to a customer just because he hands you a few pennies? Maybe you dream of buying a house or raising children, but you're sure to end your days paying off the mortgage and the college loans, and you might even die before you manage it." His words usually collided with the opinions of Mr. Muhammad, the waiter in The Arabian Nights coffee shop, who didn't like this kind of talk, and said so: "If you're not happy here, why don't you leave, brother? No one is forcing you to live in the land of the invaders, Abu Zayd!"

The new arrivals mostly agreed with Mr. Muhammad. They needled Naguib wickedly because his endless homilies and the self-pity in his eyes bored them. The younger ones didn't make any allowances for his age and experience and the decades of hard work that had worn him out. He usually answered their comments in a gentle, sad voice. "Boys, if any of you knows of a place for me back home, I wish you'd send me off on the first ship." So they let him be and the young men began to avoid sitting with him so as not to have to listen to his talk about the city's heartlessness and inhumanity, the number of vagrants and homeless people that wandered its streets, the old people in the parks neglected by children who had no time for anything but making money. He could often be heard wondering aloud about the kind of city that could produce all this human misery, this city that people called the apple of the world, a fortress of tyranny and slavery, just like all those other cities of old that had crumbled into dust.

There was no longer any place for him in the coffee shops of Bay Ridge because no one liked having him around; his talk depressed and irritated them. So he chose this corner of Park Slope, far from Bay Ridge and its Arab neighborhoods. He sat at Narak's chess table and eagerly followed the movements of the marvelous stone pieces, Snow White and Hercules and the Japanese Chu Shogi wedges.

His childlike delight in these games drew him like a magnet to the shop day after day. But most of all he enjoyed the company of his quiet Armenian friend who was often busy fiddling with his musical instruments — the oud or the violin. Layla Murad's voice wafted through the genial Armenian's shop and a feeling of peace and contentment fluttered in the folds of their shared silence. Together, they recalled the hoopoes of Nablus or that species of figbird that they used to call the Parson because of its crown of black feathers.

Naguib al-Khalili graduated with a degree in Arabic. In those days, Arabic teachers were given an extra stipend and the money allowed him to complete his studies at the High Institute of Teachers in the neighborhood of Dokki in Cairo. He and his friend Narak went to Egypt in the early 1950s and they shared an apartment on Nawal Street in Dokki for two years. On the return journey from Port Said to Beirut via Cyprus, they saw the ships, and from that day on they dreamt of crossing the oceans and seas. Finally one day they did just that and never came back.

Al-Khalili was enamored of poetry and literature and film and so he never wondered at his nephew Ziyad's passion for making movies. He would say to him in the Egyptian accent that he never entirely lost, "You're a natural, just like your uncle." Ziyad—who catches glimpses of the family's artistic future lurking behind the sacks of flour and sugar in the stockroom of The Groom's Sweets — smiles, and his uncle pats his hand affectionately. These days al-Khalili is busy with what he likes to call his life's work: a linguistic study of the most common errors in Arabic composition. He adores grammar, almost as much as he adores Layla Murad's voice and Charlie Chaplin movies.

He was famous for his ability to solve any problem related to parsing and declension, and when he was a young man everyone said that he was sure to make a good teacher one day. Naguib al-Khalili was a great admirer of the prominent Egyptian philologist Hasan Zaza. Zaza had studied classical philology in France and was proficient in more than twenty languages. He was a Jew, and the story goes that when his professor at the Sorbonne insisted that a Jew could not live safely in Egypt, Hasan Zaza—who was about to defend his dissertation proposal at the time—replied, "Come with me to Egypt and you'll see for yourself. You can walk around the streets wearing your yarmulke and people will greet you as 'Khawaga Sednaoui' or 'Khawaga Luca' and treat you with the utmost respect." Naguib al-Khalili dreamt of following in the footsteps of this Egyptian professor whose life story he knew by heart. He had a lot of other dreams too but he had ended up as a baker with a talent for making Nabulsi pastries. He considered this job to be the art of shaping the nostalgia that tugged at the heartstrings of the Lebanese and Syrians and Palestinians who lived at the edges of Brooklyn.

Al-Khalili held onto a small part of his faded dreams in the form of an old black schoolbag that he carried around everywhere. No one had a clue as to what he carried around in it all these years, or why, and the strange black bag only added to his reputation as an old eccentric. Even his old friend Narak often wondered why he held on to all those ancient books, books with titles like *Shards of Gold in the Explanation of the Language of the Arabs* and Sibawayh's *Grammar* and Ibn Malik's *Alfiya*. There was even an original manuscript he had written out in his own hand called *A Summary of Foreign and Loan Words in the Arabic Language*, with his name, Naguib al-Khalili, inscribed in a ponderous Kufic script under the title. Every morning he came to sit at the table in front of Narak's chess shop and took out his books. He would go over some complicated grammatical rules so as not to forget them, or repeat a few lines of poetry to sound out their meters, and he could often be heard cursing the exile that made him forget the rules that governed the negative and the possessive construct. Narak sits inside watching his friend as he works away at his manuscript on grammatical mistakes. Al-Khalili's normally soft voice rises a couple of notches as he calls out to ask his friend about an obscure point of classical declension. Narak, who used to be an art teacher, not a language teacher, isn't much interested in the rules of grammar. His dreams lie elsewhere. But, as everyone knows, the ship that sets sail for the east may well be driven by the wind in the opposite direction. Narak's business was on the point of collapse: customers were few and far between, as whimsical chess pieces weren't so much in demand any more. These days nobody cared about those exquisite, miniature works of art lovingly hand-sculpted by craftsmen like himself. Narak was convinced that New York had become a city inhabited by people just passing through, people who didn't give a damn about art or one-of-a-kind chess pieces. Even the number of tourists had dwindled, the winters were getting colder every year, and the warehouses were overflowing with unsold stock. Narak grieved at his son's refusal to take over the shop. The boy had begun to suggest all kinds of schemes for starting another business there. Sons wait patiently for their parents to die so they can follow their own dreams, and that's the way of the world. The thought makes Narak, who knows and loves every single piece in his shop, terribly sad. The way of the world is never fair.

Hend sits on a stoop across the street from the shop. Ziyad passes by, just as he does every evening, and says hello. Hend likes the sound of his deep, mellow voice. She likes his youthful, clean-shaven features, his nicely groomed hair, his dark, stylish clothes, and the smell of his skin. Hend likes Ziyad, but when he passes by she pretends to be busy writing something or other. Sometimes he sits down next to her and she wishes she could confess to him that she really isn't writing anything at all, that she's just pretending. She wishes she could tell him that her notebook is full of poems that she's collected, poems she wishes she had written herself. Instead she lowers her eyes and reads to him ("Come, my darling, I am the lush hyacinth soon to be plucked by autumn. . . . Take me between your hands and hold me close, covering my face with kisses"). He asks who the author is and she tells him that it's a verse from a poem by a Pashtun poetess, a woman just like her. Ziyad ignores her hint. His mind is forever on the film he's going to make. He tells her about how Quentin Tarantino, one of his favorite directors, used to work in a store just like him. True that the store was a video store—but in the end it was a store. Tarantino obviously used the opportunity to study people and watch movies and talk to his friends about cinema. Then he became a star. "That's America for you," says Ziyad, "a land of miracles." Suddenly he asks her, "Have you seen *Pulp Fiction?*" She has no idea what he's talking about so he repeats the question in Arabic and he even translates the title. She hasn't seen it, she tells him. She wants Ziyad to understand that they are interested in the same things, that she loves movies too (though she prefers Egyptian ones from the fifties), and that she especially likes the kind of movies about married couples and jilted wives. Ziyad leaves quickly before she can read the rest of her poems to him, poems she's collected for him.

Hend gazes blankly at the park frequented by old people, unserviceable people who now spend their days sipping therapeutic drinks and nibbling on sandwiches alone on empty benches. They look for a spot in the sunshine and gingerly sit down, trying hard to ignore the aches and pains of rheumatism, of loneliness and old age. They contemplate that small paradise surrounded by gigantic trees coming to life again after a long, cold winter—a cruel place in spite of its beauty for those coming to the end of their long journey. If the weather is fine, they sit and gaze at the many-colored cherry and mulberry trees, the chestnuts and oaks, while people jog around the park and young mothers with strollers congregate to spend the morning playing with their children. Hend watches her son in the chess shop from across the street.

Lilith arrives at the Armenian's shop and Naguib al-Khalili grows flustered and confused like a schoolboy with a crush as he hurriedly wipes down the chair next to him with his handkerchief. Lilith smiles and the tiny wrinkles crisscrossing her small face spring to life. She gropes for words that constantly elude her now that her memory has been snatched away by old age. Al-Khalili describes her with unparalleled zeal: "She's a real lady. There isn't another woman in this whole country as sweet or as perfect." Every day

Lilith comes to the shop and sits down opposite him wearing a spotless coat and expensive perfume and jewelry that she changes from one day to the next. She gives off an air of stately elegance and she never gets bored or interrupts his long meandering reminiscences. Her brief comments are always simple, her speech always deliberate and refined. The serious and wistful expression on her face is there thanks to the giant eraser that has wiped away most of her memory. These days she has to make a supreme effort to hold onto essential bits of information like her name, her address, and the name of her only son. She carries all her important papers with her in the pocket of her coat but she's terrified most of the time that she'll lose them or forget them, and every few minutes she feels her pocket nervously to make sure they're still there. She also keeps a small notebook where she jots down the things she wants to remember, things like her son's and grandchildren's names and the numbers of her bank accounts. She writes other things in a clear hand on little snippets of paper and then forgets where she's put them. ("Erica is my son Omar's wife. My name is Layla al-Said and they call me Lilith.") But in spite of all her precautions, her memory still fails her, and she wastes hours rummaging in her handbag and her pockets for these stray bits of paper. She is proudly and stubbornly engaged in a running battle with senility. This is why she spends a lot of time making sure every hair on her head is in place and that her coat is always spotlessly clean, and also why she prefers to remain perfectly quiet rather than open her mouth and trip up on her words.

Naguib al-Khalili, who often wonders why he feels so light and happy in Lilith's presence, watches her approaching from a distance and stands up respectfully as she draws closer. He loves talking to her. He talks and talks and she listens. He talks about the time he spent in Egypt when he was a student at the High Institute of Teachers, and about Professor Hasan Zaza and the boat from Port Said to Cyprus. He says to her, "I stayed at the Andalusia Hotel. Do you know where it is? It was one of the nicest hotels in Cairo in those days. Hot water and ice-cold water and Sudanese waiters who wore the cleanest clothes I've ever seen—cleaner even than the uniforms worn by the king's servants, madam!" Lilith smiles a little and stares dreamily into the distance. "I went to the spice market—have you been to the spice market before?" He answers his own question. "No, I guess not, you look like a real lady, so why would you frequent those old, dilapidated markets? You see, when I went to Cairo I didn't know anyone. I went with Narak." He points to his friend, bent over the strings of a violin inside the chess shop. "He was an artist back then, too, and as soon as he got to Cairo he started asking everyone where the great composer Muhammad Abd al-Wahhab lived, while I ran around looking for a place for us to rent. Of course, 'the stranger's eye is feeble,' as they say. As soon as I left the hotel I ran into a well-dressed young man who asked me if I wanted to buy an expensive Rado watch. He said that he needed the money badly and that he was willing to part with it for five pounds even though it was worth five hundred. In those days five pounds was the equivalent of more than forty Lebanese lira—enough money to live on for a whole month! But like I said, the stranger's eye is feeble, even if he's smart as a whip. And so, madam, I bought it. Then Narak came back and said, 'Naguib, they've cheated you, this watch is worthless.' Being an Armenian, Narak understood absolutely everything, but I scolded him anyway: 'You left me all this time to look for Mr. Muhammad Abd al-Wahhab's house,' I said, 'and we can't afford to stay at the Andalusia for much longer. We have to find an apartment.' And so Narak and I starting looking together for an apartment close to the center of town. We went to an agent on Nawal Street in Dokki and afterward we drank a fantastic cup of coffee at the Indiana Café. I'll never forget it my whole life."

Lilith nods her head and doesn't say a word. If she says anything, it will be something from left field like, "Oh, of course I remember Nawal . . . of course." From time to time she dabs at her face with a scented handkerchief. She checks her short, carefully cut gray hair in a little mirror or feels around in her pockets every so often to make sure that she still has the papers with her address and her son's phone number in case she gets lost. But she never loses her way. She just sits in front of Narak's shop and doesn't think of going anywhere else. She listens closely to this man who talks about faraway people and places, and smiles. Her dark pupils shine with pleasure and tears of nostalgia swim in Naguib al-Khalili's old eyes. He wipes them away with the handkerchief that he keeps in his pocket, and goes on with his stories.

"And then, madam, when the waiter at the Indiana Café (where only distinguished people used to go) told us that Abd al-Wahhab sometimes came there to meet his friends, Narak and I started going there too every day. The waiter said that he came to the café incognito, all bundled up in a black coat and hat, but that we would know him right away. 'He's tall and thin and never greets anyone and doesn't drink coffee either, only anise tea.' He told us that he was very paranoid and always pestered the waiters to make sure his glass was clean."

Layla Murad's voice comes drifting out of the shop where Narak sits listening to his friend telling the story of their lives to the strange lady called Lilith. He still likes hearing the story from Naguib's lips. Al-Khalili goes on:

"We used to spend two whole pounds on a single cup of coffee. Like I said, the Indiana Café was one of the fanciest cafés in Cairo and we were just students back then, but only bees know how to make honey, my good lady, or so I said to Narak who's sitting in the shop behind you right now. In those days he looked like Anwar Wagdi, all elegance and shining black hair—and he still does!" Naguib laughs as he looks at his old friend, then he says, "But he can't hold a candle to you, madam—'though the flower may fade, its perfume lingers on.'" Lilith smiles again and he can't tell whether she's smiling because she's understood the compliment or simply to share in his own laughter. Her decayed memory makes her shy and quiet and inscrutable. Naguib wonders whether she's even capable of putting a meaningful sentence together. Whenever she tries to share in his reminiscences about how beautiful Cairo was, for example, she only manages to repeat a random phrase whose ring happened to please her. "Beautiful . . . it was beautiful," she murmurs, then lapses into a sad silence, or a happy one; she never attempts to add anything else, and her eyes gleam mournfully. Naguib al-Khalili pauses and smiles gently into the sudden silence, then picks up the thread once again.

"Next, my good lady, I met a nice man who treated me just like his own son. We started meeting at the Rex Café downtown and going for long walks together through the city he knew so well. One day he invited me to lunch at a local grill house in the old Hussein district. I don't remember the name of the place any more, but by God, madam, I can still taste on the tip of my tongue the delicious food I ate there. Meanwhile Narak kept hanging around the Indiana and paying two pounds every day for a cup of coffee in the hopes of meeting the great composer. One day a man who fit the waiter's description—tall, silver-haired, and wearing a black coat—came in and ordered coffee. The waiter came over to tell Narak that the person he was looking for had finally arrived. Lo and behold, Narak gets up, runs over to the tall man in the black coat, covers his hand in kisses, and says, 'I've been waiting for you for a long time, maestro!' The tall man answers him with exaggerated politeness, 'I'm Abd al-Warith Isar, son!'" Naguib laughs as he glances at Narak in the back of the shop and they exchange wry smiles. "Of course you know who Abd al-Warith Isar was," he says to her. "A very great actor."

Lilith smiles that obscure smile of hers again. Perhaps she likes the story, or perhaps she's just homesick. All that al-Khalili knows about Lilith is that she's Egyptian—he knows this from the few words that she's let drop. He also knows that she has a son somewhere or other; he doesn't know what his name is, but his young American wife, Erica, sometimes comes for her at the end of the day. She wears a heavy hijab and pulls one child by the hand as she pushes a small stroller with sleeping twins in it with the other. Erica is always in a hurry. She rushes around looking for her crazy mother-in-law and declares that she's losing her mind from always having to follow her around. But Erica doesn't lose her mind because she always finds Lilith looking cool and calm as a cucumber; only her hands tremble a bit. She waits quietly for her to get up and follow her, and she never looks at Naguib al-Khalili, who watches the back of her long Islamic cloak recede into the distance as she walks away with Lilith in tow.

Lilith's apartment looks out onto the park. Her house reflects her love of elegance and her obsession with details: an antique Persian carpet, gabardine bedspreads, embroidered sheets and Arabian pillows, antique furniture, and records of all kinds. Lilith lived by herself for many years, but ever since she began to lose her memory, her son and his wife and their three children were always hovering around. Her son was Omar Azzam, the young man that the Arabs in Bay Ridge all talked about. His exemplary piety and the great wealth that God saw fit to give him were legendary. They praised him as an example of filial rectitude, especially Abd al-Karim, who liked to say, "A righteous son is the best provision against the ups and downs of this world . . . especially in this damned exile where everything fades—health and beauty and style—and the only thing you're left with is a lost and wandering mind, like Lilith's. A good boy is a blessing in those circumstances." He swears by God Almighty that if it hadn't been for her son, she would have been reduced to roaming around with the homeless people in the neighborhood and sleeping in the park.

When people asked Lilith how she came to this country, she would tell them a lot of different stories. She came from an aristocratic family—her grandfather was the minister of irrigation in the cabinet of Adli Yakan, the leader of the Free Constitutionalists. She had never been what people call a beautiful woman. She was petite and thin and dark-complexioned. She religiously followed all the latest fashions and bought all the latest records, especially

Frank Sinatra and Liza Minnelli. She loved to dance too. She married early and got pregnant right away. Her husband was a famous doctor with a big private clinic in Bab al-Luq. His practice was frequented by movie stars and all of Cairo's elite families. He had been trained in France and was related to Abd al-Wahhab Azzam—one of the most important Arab intellectuals of the twentieth century according to many.

Lilith had everything she could possibly want, but happiness is a mysterious and wayward thing. People talk a lot about the particular madness of women, but they had never seen a woman as mad as Lilith before. Lilith lived in a small mansion on the banks of the Nile in the suburb of Garden City. Her life was as ordered and picturesque as an oil painting. Her husband spoiled her no end (he called her his "little kitten") and his family often reproached him for giving her too much freedom. "Lilith is an artist and an important society lady," he would chuckle on these occasions. "She isn't a little girl any more." She would sit in the sun at the Sporting Club wearing her Jackie Kennedy sunglasses, or ride horses and go for long swims in the pool in one of her many designer bathing suits, or go to cocktail parties and mingle with famous actresses at runway shows. Then she gave birth to her only son, Omar, whom she named after Omar Sharif in the hope that he too would become a famous actor one day. She had adored his last film with Barbara Streisand, *Funny Girl*, and like all the girls of her class, she was crazy about anything to do with Hollywood and Broadway.

The birth of her son changed her dramatically, even though she had plenty of help raising him: his paternal grandmother devoted all her time to the boy and there was an army of nannies in the house. Lilith refused to nurse the child in order not to ruin her breasts and she rarely took him in her arms. She grew headstrong and sullen. She smoked a lot and slept all the time, refusing to see her son or her husband or anyone for that matter. She would rage and cry for no apparent reason. Her husband turned the rooms on the roof of the house into a pretty studio for her to paint in and he pruned the jasmine bush so that its branches would cover the walls with fragrant blossoms. He kept her company every evening and he sent for the latest records to quench her thirst for music. Their life together would have seemed ideal if not for people's gossip about the husband's many affairs. Lilith never once discussed this subject with him. She was after all a refined society lady who looked down on such trivial matters, but she gradually lost her vivacity, her joy in the world, and a sense of her place in it. One spring evening when a gentle breeze shook the jasmine blossoms loose and made them fall to the ground and give off their delicate scent, Lilith stood at the window of her room and realized that she could no longer pretend to be happy. A record turned in the gramophone and Frank Sinatra sang about learnin' the blues.

She had no idea why she suddenly burst into tears or where this feeling of longing that shook her had come from. There was no other man in her life; she never even thought about love any more. Perhaps it was the ache in Sinatra's voice that moved her so. She smoked cigarette after cigarette and felt her heart breaking. That night she dreamt of a train like the one in *Anna Karenina*. She had no idea where this train would take her or where its journey would end—a train that never stopped at any stations or complained of its loneliness.

That evening as she stood at the window of her room, her forehead pressed against the glass, listening to the song over and over, she made her decision. Her studio looked out onto the courtyard where the washing and cooking were done. The evening breeze ruffled her son's little garments hanging out to dry. The line was heavy with clothes—her delicate peignoirs and the nursing brassieres that smelled of milk and bleach. The breeze whispered plaintively and Lilith walked out of her room. Her husband was drinking his coffee in the balcony overlooking the river. She watched him sitting there in his elegant suit, his hair gleaming with health and well-being, then she gazed at the white sails of a felucca passing by on the river. She sat down opposite him silently and his gentle smile made her hesitate for a moment. She lit a cigarette to ward off the melancholy breeze that whispered to her, then she faced him squarely.

"I'm leaving. I can't bear this life any more."

He didn't ask her where she would go or why. His reply was brief. "My son is staying here with me."

She nodded her head. "Understood."

Lilith packed her bags and disappeared. They say that the husband sent her a generous sum of money every month and that she sent postcards and photos or records and sometimes long letters from New York, or New Orleans, or Los Angeles in return. He sent her photographs of her son on his birthdays, and later, school photographs so that she could see what he looked like as he grew up. They say that her family was furious with her at first, but that they eventually forgave her as time went by. They say that she saw her son again a few times in different cities; that she was constantly drawing his portrait; that she was studying at Princeton. People said a lot of things about Lilith, but you can't always believe what people say. Some claimed that they had spotted her in the company of a well-known bohemian painter in New York, or that she had covered her body in tattoos and taken to smoking dope and sleeping on the streets of Harlem and went around calling herself a genius. Others said that she worked as a secretary at a small Jewish press in Williamsburg, designing covers for cheap books and posters for amateur theater productions. People said all sorts of crazy things to ease their own burning curiosity, but no one knew the truth. Lilith tried to write her memoirs a number of times but she couldn't. Her memory had already begun to disintegrate and by then no one cared about the truth any more.

Her son Omar came to America years later to study engineering. She opened the door and there he was. He took her in his arms and together they tried to forget a lot of things, as though all those years had never come between them. He lays his head in her lap and calls her Lulu. She tells him all about her life, which is no longer important or interesting. She tells him how she used to paint like a madwoman and go to the theater and to art openings. She says things like "A long time ago before your time, Omar—New York was like such and such." Lilith no longer did any of the things she told Omar about. Now she preferred to take walks in the nearby park or to watch over the basil and wild mint plants that grew in her window. Her son Omar would come and then disappear for long stretches, and she would say to herself, "He's a young man living his life." Sometimes he stayed with his friends or traveled to places she knew nothing about. She believed that it was his life to live as he liked, and she never interfered. She also believed that time changes everything and a person never knows what they want until they know.

The boy who had come to America to study engineering began to experiment with acting and singing. He joined a band and traveled around half the country with them. Lilith didn't notice when he started to pray all the time because whenever he tried to talk to her, she would gaze off abstractedly into the distance with a strange expression on her face. Omar began to notice that she spoke and moved about less and less. Her son would lay his head in her lap and say, "What's wrong, Lulu? Why are you so far away?" If he had understood anything about the way of the world, he would have known that her soul had embarked on a long journey to a place only old people can see. There was no one to explain this to Omar and so her forgetfulness frightened him. Her son hugs her close. He's all grown up now and married to a young, fair-skinned girl called Erica who converted at the Islamic Center on Atlantic Avenue in Brooklyn. He married her according to the law of God and his Prophet, and now he's a prosperous entrepreneur in the construction and demolition business and he makes a point of hiring unemployed Arab immigrants. He's also part-owner of a string of those grocery stores they call 'delis,' and his partners are mostly Yemenis.

Omar did a lot of charity work in the community. He started giving his mother Qurans as presents in the hope that she might pick one up and read God's word a little before going to sleep. He talked to her a lot about the Quran and how reading from it regularly would soothe away her sorrows and strengthen her memory. The remedy for forgetting, he would say to her, is forswearing sin and disobedience to God. But poor Lilith couldn't even remember her sins. He brought her saffron as a remedy but she brushed it aside, saying that she had no need for it. And yet she did need it, and she feared this need. She feared that she would end up like the old people on the street, with dirty clothes smelling of the body's final collapse. She began to change her clothes constantly, but she would forget that she had just changed them and change them again. She got into the habit of washing her hands every few minutes. She would sit at the window that looked out onto the park, lean her head against the glass, and let her thoughts wander far away as she listened to her old Sinatra records.

Omar decided to perform the pilgrimage to Mecca. "I've forgiven you, Mother, and I want God to forgive you too," he said to her. "Come with me." He wept as he spoke. It was the first time she had heard her son say such things about her. She never really understood that she had broken his heart all those years ago and that he had lived his whole life desperately needing her to repent of it. He still remembers after all this time, she wondered to herself; and then she got angry.

"So you want me to turn in circles around the Ka'ba? Son, I have no patience for turning in circles and I don't like your innuendos. You go. If He wants to forgive me, He'll forgive me."

It was a constant struggle to stay as she was. She had never been conscious of committing the vague sins he begged her to atone for. Back then, she was still capable of living alone, of sitting on a park bench by herself and jotting down in a little notebook the sentences that she hoped would eventually become her memoirs. But she never got farther than the title. Her memory rebelled against the blank white pages. She was incapable of conjuring all the little details that make up a life. She turned in circles around herself in a final, stubborn attempt to assert her independence. She pasted old photos of herself in Washington Square Park on the blank pages of the notebook. In one photo her hair is short and wild like Liza Minnelli's and her bare arms are covered in tattoos. In another, she has African braids and she's showing off a tattoo on her back that says "I'm free" in English. A third photo shows her sitting on the sidewalk of Thompson Street, a cigarette dangling from her mouth.

The notebook meanwhile remained innocent of writing. She sketched one self-portrait after another in charcoal on the white pages, images of a woman with hollow cheeks and a long nose and curly black hair, hands clasped to her withered breast—a solitary woman on the threshold of winter.

Brooklyn Bridge

The hanging bridge sleeps, surrendering to the footsteps of the passersby and the tourists and immigrants who have walked across it for a century or more. Small boats called ferries pass underneath it on the river that separates Brooklyn from Manhattan. Before the bridge was built the ferries were the only means of crossing to the other side. The Fulton Street and Wall Street ferries still carry photo-snapping tourists and pleasure-seekers from one bank to the other. The bridge is like a hardy old ship battered by time, welcoming the legions of unemployed on sunny winter mornings and drawing noisy activists protesting about every kind of issue, from the environment and racial discrimination to gay rights and health insurance. The processions all start out from the bridge and head to City Hall in Manhattan and sometimes they move in the other direction toward downtown Brooklyn.

The bridge casts a glittering mantle of enchantment over Brooklyn with all its contradictions. Hend walks across it at night for the first time, Ziyad at her side chattering away about Tarantino and the film he's about to start shooting. He laughs suddenly and Hend's heart contracts painfully. Venus has been fast asleep in her zodiac for the past few days. She marvels at the thing called love, its unexpectedness, and its breathtaking absurdity. She resolves to play out the first and final scenes of her short life in the manner of a diva. As a young girl she was convinced that she resembled a few of them. She had always been a passably good actress with a talent for melodrama and histrionics. She was passionate and willful even though life hadn't given her the chance to express these traits to the full. When Ziyad told her that he was looking for an Arab woman to act in his short film about a family of Arab immigrants, she seized the chance to do something she had always dreamed of doing. Even when he told her that the only remuneration was a hot meal, Hend enthusiastically agreed.

Ziyad, tall and captivating, stops halfway across the bridge and tells her the story in his strong Palestinian accent. It's about a girl whose father beats her because she's forgotten how to speak in Arabic. Whenever she tries to say something, she stutters and stumbles and falls back in frustration on 'the F word' (an obscenity that means 'you and your language can go to hell'). The father, whose own dreams lie in ruins, named his daughter after his beloved mother, and he absolutely forbids her to talk to boys. When the girl gets older she chooses a new name for herself. The father catches her kissing a boy on the Brooklyn Bridge one day. He drags her away by the hair, swearing by everything he holds sacred to kill her. At home, he forces her to take off her tight jeans and kicks her over and over. "Whore! Slut!" he screams. Then he takes off his leather belt and beats her on her legs and buttocks as she screams in pain and fury. The police come and haul the father off, and in the last scene, the heroine runs hysterically across the Brooklyn Bridge, her desperate mother running after her and calling out in vain.

At first she didn't realize that her part in the film would be confined to one short scene. Ziyad tried to soften the blow. "It's the most important scene in the movie!" Hend nodded her head and glanced at Diana Kirdashi, the eldest daughter of Abd al-Karim who spent his days in The Arabian Nights Café and distributed leaflets about the coming Day of Judgment. Diana wore a pair of torn jeans and a white t-shirt with "I Love New York" printed on it. Hend, on the other hand, was dressed in a long Pakistani salwar kameez and her head was covered in a shawl of the kind worn by pitiful Muslim mothers in old movies. She was supposed to run after the heroine and shout, "Daughter, daughter!" with a mixture of conflicted emotions—anguish, love, fear, and disappointment. It had to show in the cast of her eyes and the hoarseness of her voice. Ziyad told her that the shawl had to slip as she ran, uncovering her heaving breast and letting the sun glint off her gray hair.

They had to repeat the scene more than once because she kept getting it all wrong and stumbling on her long clothes as she ran after her supposed daughter, and Ziyad complained that she didn't look terrified enough. He tried to explain the scene to her more clearly: "You're a mother who is about to lose her daughter to suicide. Just concentrate your emotions on what that might feel like. Please, this is the most important scene in the film." Hend nods to show that she understands him—even more than he imagines. But she doesn't like this role. She doesn't want to be anybody's mother. For once, she just wants to be herself; she wanted Ziyad to see her as a woman in her own right, to see that she could play other roles than the one he had in mind.

Hend had always secretly wanted to be an actress and dreamt of playing the starring role. As a child she used to stand in front of the mirror and playact. She would cock her eyebrows like Faten Hamama in *A Happy Day* and declare out loud, "Shall I bring you the coat now or in a little while, sir?" She would talk to herself in a loud theatrical voice and, at the end of the 'movie,' kiss the image reflected in the mirror. Her mother mocked this secret conversation with her cinematic ghosts. "You must be possessed by demons, child, staring at yourself night and day like that in the mirror. What would you be doing if you were actually pretty?" So she spent even more time in front of the mirror, her one solace and refuge. She daubed her face with milky white lotions and stole her mother's fuchsia lipstick from the vanity drawer so that she could paint Layla Murad lips in the shape of a small deep red heart over her own. She took off her blouse and cupped the breasts that hadn't fully appeared yet as she sang her favorite song, "I'm in

Love and I Have No Regrets; People, Advise Me!" It was a song that she had heard her grandmother the Guest sing many a time as she washed her plastic sandals on the roof of her grandfather Muqawi Abul Karmat's house.

She puts her ear to the transistor radio and repeats Shadia's lines from the radio soap opera *Bitter Honey*. The heroine was a siren who seduced men with her hoarse, lascivious voice. Shadia's voice dripped bitter honey but it wasn't as moving or provocative as the part called for. It was low and silky, and full of gentle sensuality, a dreamy voice that sounded like Zubeida Tharwat's in the movie *A Night in My Life*. Hend wished that she could escape and hide like Zubeida Tharwat in the movie—then they would miss her desperately and search frantically everywhere for her.

She buys *Star* magazine and gazes, moonstruck, at her favorite heroines. She tries to copy their hairstyles. She really was a great actress. Her family was constantly rediscovering this talent of hers whenever she flew into a rage and tied up her clothes in a cloth bundle and swore that she wasn't their daughter, that they had probably found her abandoned some place or another. "Those eyes of yours are full of crocodile tears," her mother said to her. "What am I going to do with you? You're driving us both crazy. Dear God, instead of a daughter You've cursed me with this endless heartache."

Radios soon become a thing of the past and her father bought the first TV set (Arab Toshiba) in all of Pharaoh's Hills. They put it in the living room between the two balconies, and Hend watched all three episodes of the wildly popular soap opera called *The Victim—The Departure—The Fugitive*. A group of townswomen quietly gathered around the TV in the living room, watching the show like her and crying. She tried to act out the most moving scenes, and most of the time her tears were real. She grew moody and quarrelsome, at times like a changeful breeze, at others like a raging bull, depending on the role she was playing that particular day.

When she grew a bit older, she took on the role of 'the saint.' She wore herself out praying and talking about sin and scandal. She lost weight and went around with a skinny Christ-like body covered in rags that exhibited her piety for anyone who cared to notice. She walked down the dusty paths of Pharaoh's Hills, charitably bestowing greetings on the people who lived in the cemeteries. She stood under the mulberry tree at the crossroads waiting for her friends to join her from the nearby estates, their shoes caked in mud and dust as they made their way to school. She never raised her lowered eyes in fear of temptation. During play period, she sat in the farthest corner of the classroom so as not to be noticed, shrinking into herself, practically sticking to the window so that she could gaze out at the desolate cemetery next door and contemplate sin and death while the other girls spent the whole period singing and dancing. Zaynab—otherwise known as Zuba—was one of those girls. Her father had come to Pharaoh's Hills from Cairo and she was always boasting about being from the tough neighborhood of Bulaq. She was plump and fair-skinned and she wore a pink blouse that revealed the flesh between her ivory breasts. All the male teachers constantly stared at that very spot and considered it an ode to feminine beauty. The female teachers scolded her and told her to button up her blouse but she would just laugh her deep, throaty laugh and say, "I swear they're just jealous of me." The female teachers weren't the only ones. Hend was bitterly jealous of her too.

Hend always sat apart contemplating the cemetery and fantasizing about a slender, movie-star figure with voluptuous, shimmying curves. Zuba carried a case in her pocket with a pair of tweezers and a roll of sewing thread, always ready to do the eyebrows of the envious teachers and students for five piasters. She sat in the very front of the classroom because she adored the spotlight. The male teachers were all obsessed with her in one way or another—the attitudes of some of them ranged from fatherly to brotherly, while some of the others lusted after her openly. Zuba would laugh and wiggle her eyebrows at them, drawing them further into her snares. In place of a heart she had an enticing pair of breasts and she easily did without the handful of feelings that make a person laugh or cry. During free periods like arts and crafts or home economics, Zuba would leave the door slightly ajar and dance. She really knew how to shake her belly in a way that rivaled the infamous ghawazi dancers that Muhammad Ali banished from the city of Cairo. She pranced around and wiggled her body from head to toe. The echo of the rhythmic drum beats never got as far as the principal's office, which was tucked far away behind the classrooms.

Why did they all envy her, Hend wondered, when she had freely chosen the role of the playful and erotic public dancer? Zuba was extremely talented, as she herself liked to say. She was an expert at waxing women's private parts and painting their eyes with kohl and their nails with cheap, flashy red polish that brought out the enticing whiteness of their hands. The 'saint' was content to observe all this with frigid contempt. She extracted a deep moral and religious lesson from the cemetery outside the window, though she knew the rumors that circulated about Zuba and the cemetery, how she charged the boys twenty-five piasters to take off her clothes in the dark between the tombs so they could gape at her naked flesh. And whenever the competition between Zuba and her rivals exploded out into the open as it sometimes did, they called her "the graveyard girl," because the tombs were a place full of worms and corruption.

Zuba puts her hand on her hip and lets out a string of obscenities. She's from Bulaq, as she keeps telling everyone. "Who do you think I am, you mommy's girls?" The girls stare at her open-mouthed while the art teacher stares at the floor in silence. He's a pious man who fears God—so pious that he forbids them to draw human beings, or any creature with a soul for that matter. Instead he makes them draw landscapes that illuminate the Creator's infinite wisdom. The art teacher doesn't like Zuba and he doesn't pay any attention to her, so Zuba summarily dismisses him as "a pansy." "You think he's a man?" she asks defiantly. Hend glares at her. "He's respectable and he has a romantic spirit. Not the type of person you'd be familiar with." Zuba laughs. "Girl, you're the romantic one," she says insinuatingly. She knows that Hend has a crush on the art teacher and that her exaggerated interest in cemeteries is her way of impressing him with her piety. Hend doesn't bother to ask how Zuba managed to discover her secret passion. Everyone knows that the art teacher sent her a letter in which he addressed her as "my little kitten." The letter was for her alone and Hend accordingly hid it in her bundle of secret papers. Despite the letter, they both stuck to their habitual roles of saint and mentor. When he talked he never looked at her. He looked at Angele—who shared her bench—instead, and said things like, "You're a good girl, Angele. You're a saint, an angel come down from heaven." Everyone knew his words were really meant for Hend because Angele was dark-skinned and overweight and not very attractive. The girls in the class looked at Hend with new eyes. They started calling her Mariam Fakhr al-Din, the dreamy, romantic movie star with the sweet and innocent face who trails catastrophe in her wake. One day, Zuba suddenly disappeared along with the art teacher, and rumors began to circulate that he had gotten her pregnant and run away with her. A number of years later they came back to the town as an officially married couple with a bunch of legally begotten children.

After their disappearance, Hend was filled with jealousy and shame. She wished she could hide behind Angele's huge body and shut her ears against the sarcasm and jibes of her classmates. She started to hate the role of 'saint.' She decided that it was stupid and endlessly boring and she began to try on the role of 'victim' instead. She told herself that she must be a victim, just like her mother, who did nothing but sob and sniffle and say "yes" and "All right" all day long.

When she sat in the balcony and sang to herself, her mother reminded her of Layla Murad. There was one song in particular that she would sing to her husband—provided he was in the mood of course—when he laid his head in her lap. She would run her hand over his hair affectionately and sing: *Who can compare to him? How sweet and beautiful he is!* He laughs and she goes on, *Marvelous spring rose, carnations, oh carnations.* He kisses her on the lips in front of the playing children and for those brief moments her mother becomes the leading lady and her heart swells with happiness. She sings as she cooks and cleans and her voice rings out with the sweetness of a woman who knows that she is loved and that the time for love is, alas, too short. But when she gets angry, she takes on the role of the victim weeping and complaining about her trials and tribulations. Hend learned her own role in life from her mother, especially after she became a mother herself. She spent her entire adolescence and youth in the belief that victims like herself had no will of their own, that they were objects of pity or compassion who played crucial roles in stories and films because they spoke to the hidden cruelty in the hearts of men and women. But one day Hend finally rose up in rebellion. She kicked the battered glass door and said to her brothers, who had by then grown into men: "I'm going to marry him whether you like it or not"—an immortal line in countless old movies. The family elders who solemnly gathered in their white Bedouin headdresses to discuss this unheard-of insurrection declared, "Let her go to hell, we don't want any scandals."

She became a lovely, refined bride and her life turned into a Zahrit al-Ula movie: from now on she would play the role of the young, abandoned wife. She went back to the role of victim and deliberately courted the pity of one and all. Whenever she shut herself up in her room, her husband would say to her, "You just can't live without some melodrama for a single day, can you?" But she was smart enough to know that he had gotten it backward. Melodrama was part and parcel of the way of the world, like birth and death and sorrow and boredom.

In the end she decided that the most appropriate ending to that particular movie should be spectacular and open-ended, so she ran away for good. And now here she is coming down from the Brooklyn Bridge after finishing her scene and discovering the truth about her acting abilities at one fell swoop, with no makeup or lighting to keep up the illusion of a lifetime. All she had to do was run after a little whore pretending to be her daughter—the very role that she had spent her whole life trying to avoid. She thinks to herself that her life has been nothing but a series of adaptations of old movies. She tells herself that the many costumes she's worn at one time or another were never sized to fit her soul. She remembers the red knit dress with the three green flowers that she used to wear as a child. She remembers that the color of her school uniform was a dull gray, rather than the standard navy blue. Gray suited her because she wanted to be different, to declare her superiority. Sometimes she would throw open the doors of her mother's wardrobe and examine the flounced dresses that looked like the ones Layla Murad wore in the movie *The Flirtation of Girls*. Her fingers lovingly lingered on the loose silky cloches, the double cloche cambered and arranged in a perfect oval around the elegant neckline. Her mother, who always complained of her aching back, no longer wore any of them, and Hend dared to hope they would be hers one day. Her mother's serial pregnancies had left their mark on her body and the abandoned dresses became a shrine to her aristocratic lineage and the days of her first slenderness, as well as a memorial to her fashionable Armenian dressmaker who lived in Tal'at Harb Street in Cairo and made clothes for all the great actresses of the day. Now her mother was content to make an annual trip to the department stores Sednaoui and Shamla, because they were close by and their prices were reasonable. She would cautiously inquire about the price of the fine cotton linen, but she always bought the cambric printed with miniature flowers because it was cheaper and the piqué because it was tough and naturally stain-resistant.

Hend follows Umm Hanan around with yards of the cheap fabric. The seamstress turns them into clothes that constantly come back to her for alterations. "Mama says can you shorten the sleeves, mama says can you lengthen this hem, mama says can you take in the waist . . . ?" Umm Hanan finally loses patience. "You think I don't have anything to do but take care of you?" she explodes. "Go tell your mother I don't do alterations any more!"

Her mother took care of everything—that's why Hend's clothes all looked the same when she was a young girl: modest knee-length skirts and blouses with three-quarter sleeves to keep the sun from burning her arms but also so they wouldn't get wet when she washed the dishes. All her blouses and dresses had to be high-necked because, as her mother always said, no daughter of hers went around with bare bosoms like actresses and prostitutes. And so Hend wore those clownish dresses made of piqué that turned her body into a neutral, shapeless thing. From time to time she tore them up or packed them away for her great escape and on these occasions her mother would say to her, "You're driving me crazy! Are you a girl or some kind of evil spirit?"

The rending of clothes was a family tradition that she was careful to keep up, especially after she got married. Faten Hamama performed a brilliant version of this ritual in Hend's favorite film *The Thin Line*, where she played the role of a furious, abandoned woman. Hend used to take solace in the remarkable fact that even the lovely and talented Faten Hamama could play a character like that. In the end she took to wearing an embroidered abaya because she was 'the daughter of Bedouin Arabs' after all, the descendant of some tribe called the Tiyaha Tribe whose women all hid behind black veils. Her grandmother used to hang her black gowns on a washing line stretched between two nails in her room because she claimed that the moths devoured everything piled up in closets. She would point proudly to each of the gowns hanging on the line: "Velvet from Mecca, Yemeni satin, Indian silk." Hend never saw her wearing her Indian silk or her Yemeni satin because she only ever went out to attend the funerals of the old women in the neighborhood. She died suddenly in her turn and the other old women put on their scented black gowns and sat at her wake, mournfully reeling off the virtues of the departed Guest. Toward the end of her life, Hend's mother also took to wearing a black abaya whenever she went out of the house on one of her rare trips to the doctor. "Well, it's just something to cover yourself with after all . . . ," she would sigh.

Hend runs her hand through her hair as she walks across the bridge. She remembers how it used to be long and black when she was a child, hiding her small skinny body and consuming all her strength. Her mother used to braid it into a single, long braid. She would get angry as she pulled and twisted the unruly mass of hair. She complained that it was like horse hair rather than human hair. Hend had no idea what horse hair was like; all she knew was that it hurt when her mother combed it. She didn't like wearing it in two braids either. Her mother did it that way sometimes because it supposedly warded off the evil eye of the enviers. In old photos Hend stares gravely at the camera with her hair done in those two long braids. She is not beautiful. She looks out from the photograph still and quiet, obscured by the long hair that she inherited from no one. Her mother used to say that she had longed to have hair like Miss Nadia's when she was pregnant with her. Hend discovered that Miss Nadia was the music teacher who had come to Pharaoh's Hills before she was born and taught her mother how to crochet hats. She was the one who knitted the red dress that Hend always saw in the family photos, and she was apparently the one who had bequeathed her that long, ponderous mass of black hair, the like of which they had never seen in the annals of the family. Miss Nadia left Pharaoh's Hills and went back to her own country ages ago, but her name would always come up whenever the subject of Hend's hair did.

When she grew up she left the braids behind and took to wearing her hair in a huge bun pinned tight with clips because whenever she let it hang loose down her back her mother would say to her curtly, "Gather it up." So she gathered it up since it hid her thin face anyway. She wished she could cut it off but didn't, because she knew that her mother would then say something like, "But your hair's your only good feature!" The men who loved her were also quite open about their obsession with her hair, and she began to hate it. On many a sleepless night as she lay struggling to ignore the painful swelling in her breasts and the acrid smell of milk that assailed her nostrils, she would suddenly realize that her baby had wound his little fist tightly in her long thick hair and fallen asleep with a blissful expression on his face. She would spend hours trying to free the strands from between the viselike grip of his fingers, but he always woke up with a start and wound his hand in the mass even more tightly. (He still does it before falling asleep, while she dreams every night that she's hacking away at it with a pair of scissors.) In that period of her life, her hair became a reliable barometer of the generally wretched state of her emotional health. It fell out in clumps, leaving bare patches like ulcers behind. It grew thin and frizzy as a result of her many fits of jealousy and bouts of depression, as though sharing in the wasteland of her loneliness. Her hair determined many of the roles she had played in her life.

When the Arabic teacher came back from Yemen—having performed the pilgrimage to Mecca and repented to God—he informed her that her hair was sinful, and so she hid it underneath veils of fear. The Arabic teacher was an expert at detecting temptation wherever it was to be found: this girl's chest was too big and she should cover it completely, or the outlines of that student's rear end were too high and round under her uniform and therefore she should take off the belt around her waist and wear a loose skirt. He was quite practiced at pointing out the differences between those still growing bodies. Hend covered her hair and drew closer to God. She covered it because each and every strand was sure to lead her straight to the fires of hell. She cut it short, then regretted having done so because now she could no longer recognize the girl looking out at her from the mirror.

Her hair was the battleground of many wars. She cuts off a piece of it and presents it to the one she loves, a small token of her undying troth. Her mother pulls her around by her hair. She says things like "Do you think you can just let it all hang loose like that?" Hend threatens to set it on fire if they don't let her marry of her own free will, to make her own decisions for once. She starts to wear it down, in one cascading mass, liberating it from the casing of cloth and fear. It falls out in clumps after each scene with her husband. It piles up on pillows and in the teeth of combs and in the corners of her father's house. Grandmother Zaynab—God rest her soul—used to gather it into cloth pouches and bury it in the sand to protect her from the work of evil spirits once she realized that Hend's stars were crossed and that she was the object of the evil eye of the enviers. But that didn't stop her being miserable. She began to suffer from migraines. The pain emanated from underneath her scalp and the pills that she constantly swallowed were no use at all.

Her mother takes her head in her lap and holds her close to stop her crying. She tells her with the wisdom of a woman who knows everything there is to be known about migraines and aching backs and the fickleness of men, "To hell with him, my daughter, men are good for nothing but headaches. Are you going to kill yourself fretting? Forget him." Hend tries but she doesn't forget him.

She stands gazing in the mirror at the strands of hair that fall away when she tugs at them with her hand. They lie in stray piles on the floor like a hodgepodge of memories waiting to be gathered up and tossed in the waste bin. She neither cries nor rejoices. She only feels that she's free now, just as she had always longed to be. She runs across the Brooklyn Bridge in the black coat that she picked out carefully one day from the rack in a used clothing store: a coat that expresses her fashion sense, loose and dark like a shapeless sack. It adds a few extra years to her age and generously conceals all the things that Hend wishes to conceal. Her hair is short and black, her step hesitant, her dress modest and dignified, her gaze lowered. Some of the passersby on Seventh Avenue mistake her for an Orthodox Jew and some even hand her leaflets about Temple Beth Elohim and call her "my little Jewish lady." She smiles to herself because this always happens to her whenever she walks past the old watch-repair stores in Williamsburg or on Third Avenue. People in that neighborhood always mistake her for a Mizrahi Jew. The Latinos too think she's one of them, because of her full figure and her black hair, and the Indians look at her kohl-painted eyes and nod their heads at her affectionately ("Kashmiri?" they ask her), while other immigrant communities claim her as one of their own. She walks along Seventh Avenue in the long black coat that transforms her into someone else, anyone else. She looks at herself in the mirror but can't find the little girl who used to trek past the agricultural cooperative and the Muqawi Primary School to join the dusty procession of gypsies. All she sees is a strange woman who looks like her.

The Cold Season

From time immemorial the Arabs have attached many meanings to the wind, perhaps more than it can bear. They took it as a good omen, but also a bad one, and they gave it countless names: the poison wind, the wind of good tidings, the lunatic wind. It carried scents across the deserts and prophesied the arrival of travelers; it warned tyrants and laid waste to villages of sin till they became like the hollow stumps of palm trees. They charged it with their dreams and desires, for the wind carried the beloved's sighs and brought tidings of the coming of the rains. They said, "The wind plants fear in the heart of the seafarer" and "The winds are hostage to His command," for they believed that everything that happens in this world is predestined and subservient to the Supreme Will, against which men are powerless to act.

The khamasin winds descended upon the Heights in spring. They ruffled the sands on top of the hill where Hend sat with her father in front of the reception house. The leaves fell from the camphor tree and the air grew thick with dust and the smell of camphor and death. Her father said to her, "This is the *yud* wind." She didn't know what the word meant, so she said nothing. "The Persians and the people of Khurasan called it *yud*—the wind of longing. Do you know why they gave it that name? Because of the souls of the dead. The dead constantly long for those they've left behind in this world, so they come back in the form of a gentle breeze and take away a few of their loved ones, then go back to the place they came from." Hend was frightened. Her father went on. "Do you know why they rub the bodies of dead people with camphor leaves after washing them?" Hend shook her head, not wanting to hear the rest of the story. For the first time, the tone of her father's voice filled her with fear, and the faraway look in his eyes made her shiver. She begged him to tell her the story of 'Hend the daughter of King Nu'man' instead.

The father puts his hand on her shoulder and they walk side by side. Hend was his only companion now that Shamil the pharmacist had left for Libya and Emile the principal had gone to join his relatives in Canada. The new civil servants in town weren't interested in the reception house and its host, and most of the parties in local disputes now preferred to solve their problems in the mosque according to the laws of religion and the ways of the Prophet. Fatma al-Qarumiya had donned a long black veil and taken to sitting on the ground in front of the Nur Mosque selling musk oil, siwak toothpicks, Qurans, and pamphlets on prophetic medicine with detailed cures for ailments like asthma and migraine. Fatma al-Qarumiya's immense body squats squarely on the ground. She looks like a seated camel, a mass of flesh that shakes when she lets out her famous laugh and says to passersby, "What can I do, cousin? I'm a just businesswoman, I buy and sell whatever I can get in the market."

In spite of the rapid urbanization that had swept through Pharaoh's Hills, there were still desolate rocky heights and woods crawling with scorpions. Hend isn't sure exactly when her father started to develop an interest in the life cycle of insects, or when he began to collect with a pair of iron tongs the tiny yellow scorpions that came out at night from their lairs around the Heights. She would walk next to him carrying a fluorescent flashlight and when she pointed it at one of the creatures, it instantly froze. Her father caught the scorpions with the tongs and put them carefully in an airtight glass jar. He kept the jar in the Guest's old bedroom in the reception house. The Guest's scent still lingered on in that abandoned room. Hend sniffed the familiar perfume: a mixture of olive oil soap, musk, peppermint, and the camphor that she used to put in the folds of her gowns. When the Guest passed away her gowns grew shabby and faded, of course, but the strong smell remained, drifting out every time they opened the door to her abandoned bedroom.

Her father goes into the room, followed by Hend. He places the glass jars containing the scorpions on the windowsill. Hend stares at the wide old sill where a tray with clay water jars and a small kerosene lamp used to sit. The Guest used to hang strings of chili peppers, grapes, and figs to dry on its wood frame. She often left plates of stewed beans and kishk sitting out on the sill to keep them cool and fresh. Hend gazes out at the Heights through the window, the window that let in the cold north wind. She spots Venus gleaming in the twilight sky. The Guest used to mark the passing hours and the change of seasons as she sat at that window basking in the summer breeze, which she claimed was more exquisite than the fans of Paradise. Hend stands watching her father as he transfers the yellow sand scorpions into larger transparent pickle jars, then carefully seals them and leaves them on the windowsill. He shuts the door fast behind him as he tells her about how he is on the verge of discovering a cure for diabetes made from scorpion venom. Hend feels happy to be helping her father on such an important project, but also because he spends much more time with her now that all his old friends have gone away. They went on long walks together—from the reception house to the Heights, and from the Hill Estate back home, and they always stopped to greet the migrant workers whom they passed in the fields. They spent hours every day catching spiders to feed to the scorpions. He explained his theory to her: a small injection of scorpion venom strengthens the body's immunity. He also told Hend—who wanted to believe him—that Bedouin Arabs like him knew these things because they were natives of the desert. The little scorpion farm on the windowsill became their special secret. Hend learned to tell the difference between the males and females just by looking. She had mostly gotten over her initial fear of them, until the first time she saw them mating in a weird dance that went on for hours.

It was a scene that she would never forget for as long as she lived. The male scorpion scurried back and forth, revolving around the female warily in ever narrowing circles, and they turned together in a long, cautious tango without touching. The male ejected his sperm onto the ground and the female scooped it up into her abdomen with her rear legs. She puffed up slowly, enormous and satisfied, then fell perfectly still while the male ran up and down the side of the glass jar frantically searching for an exit. The impregnated female scorpion moved toward him with slow, heavy steps, her poisonous tail raised stiffly in anticipation. The male jumped around even more frantically knowing he was trapped. She caught him between her jaws and devoured him piece by piece, and once she had finished she fell into a long period of total immobility that lasted for days. Finally, the mother scorpion woke up. She carried the tiny embryos around on her back for weeks. After this period of gestation, the embryos were transformed into little scorpions that scurried rapidly around the jar much like the fleeing male. They ran up and down the sides of the jar; they ran circles around themselves. They were small and hungry and terribly excited. The mother scorpion submitted to them. The little scorpions gathered around her in a tight circle and began to feed on her body. Hend was twelve years old at the time. She started having terrifying nightmares about scorpions and began to wet herself again. Her mother scolded her father sharply: "Shame on you, the girl is unstable enough as it is and you're making her help you raise scorpions!"

For weeks after that, Hend was forbidden to join in any of her father's many projects and expeditions, from raising silkworms or hunting for black widow spiders to observing the mating habits of yellow lizards. In the end her father failed to find his cure for diabetes. He simply abandoned the experiment altogether. He stopped going to the Heights and the reception house, and he confined himself to the eastern balcony where he told her stories of the Prophet Solomon. He told her that when Solomon died and his soul went up to meet its Creator, his body remained behind, leaning on a cane. The construction of his splendid palace had not yet been completed, and Solomon's body stayed on to finish supervising the jinn who were building it. The jinn only realized he was dead when the ants had finished consuming his cane from the ground up and then the body, that had pretended to be living, immediately toppled over. Her father died in the same way the Prophet Solomon did. One day, he just toppled off his chair in the eastern balcony. The smell of camphor drifted down from the Heights and the wind passed through, carrying off his soul and leaving his body leaning on his cane and clutching at his left shoulder in terror as the death spittle trickled out of his mouth.

When the father died, the mother descended into the most profound silence. She no longer shouted at Hend, she no longer laughed or flew into rages: she just sat in the eastern balcony every evening on the wooden rocking chair, her eyes resting on the long washing line that hung between a branch of the mulberry tree and the house beam, the line that had been swinging back and forth before her eyes ever since she came from her father's house to her husband's house. On that line she had hung the silky underwear of a young bride and her white sheet stained with tears and sweat and the secretions of love. At first the scent of lavender and violets rose from the line, then, years later, the clothes that weighed it down began to smell of milk and urine and baby spittle. The line swung harder than ever under the sun, and smiled to itself.

Alone at night it stretched out between the two worlds, keeping an eye on the balcony and listening to the stories that drifted out on the evening breeze from the rush mat. During the day it took in the smell of freshly baked bread and the leftover scraps tossed to the chickens and roosters. The mother gazed at the lonely line, which, like her, was watching the swallows perched on the branches of the mulberry tree and listening for the shouts of the children as they ran underneath and tugged at it playfully. The children didn't care in the least whether it was warmed by the sun or tousled by the wind, and they never noticed the fine layer of dust that settled on it. The mother sat in the balcony watching the children grow up and move farther and farther away from her, leaving her with long wrinkles under the eyes and minute and flexible lines on the forehead, the threads of insomnia. The clothesline watches this little woman growing old in its lifetime, each of them demarcating a space of absolute solitude. They pull at each other, silence for silence. They watch each other intently like partners in a crime. The line swings back and forth with its cargo of pistachio-colored dresses and satin hair ribbons, children's socks and brassieres stained with cancerous, clotted milk. One night, the mother smiled as she sat in the balcony and watched the old line swing to and fro; then she walked into her room and shut the door behind her, and that was the end of their story together.

Hend was walking toward Fourth Avenue when the wind of longing suddenly blew up over the trees of Prospect Park, brushing against the silver and white poplars and the fragrant cypresses and oaks. Nobody usually noticed the turning of the seasons in a big city like New York where people were constantly running around, but some discerning observers did remark the exceptional movement of the planets in the heavens on that day: an alignment that astronomers say occurs every forty-five years or so. They call it *yud*, which means the Finger of God. During this period, the planets all seem to be suddenly moving backward. It's as though you were driving a car, and all the trees on the road ahead are now behind. The trees haven't really moved backward, and the planets don't either. It just looks that way. That spring, three planets moved backward and produced the alignment the old people call the wind of longing. Mercury, the planet of memory, moved into Capricorn; Saturn moved into Libra, Uranus into Pisces, and the earth shook in awe at this momentous event. People wondered in amazement how all the distant memories they had left behind long ago were now suddenly standing squarely before them. They couldn't understand why so many things that had been erased from their thoughts were once again haunting them. The past became the present and it swept one and all away with the force of its violent return. People gathered around Jojo the fortune teller on Fourth Avenue, with her ancient Egyptian scarab and her statue of a clay frog representing the god Sekhmet, guardian of the western tombs in the Valley of the Kings. And though her Russian friend Emilia told them not to believe anything she said ("They're just a bunch of old wives' tales!"), they did not doubt that the planets that were now gathered to draw the image of creation had truly provoked the fragrance that filled the park with its bittersweet scent. They congregated in circles to watch the total eclipse of the moon over their city and talk about the stars and horoscopes and bad luck. The park had burst into flower like never before, its trees blooming with life, their white blossoms carpeting the soft ground. The scent of longing made people fan out in groups on stoops and sidewalks and lawns and exchange greetings with random strangers. The foreigners among them were suddenly seized by an urgent need to talk about their distant home countries.

Narak, who was sitting in his shop going over the accounts, picked up his violin and fell into a deep sleep. Just before he dropped off, he said to his friend, "I can smell the wind of Paradise, Naguib." Naguib al-Khalili chuckled, one eye on the lovers kissing on the green lawn and the other watching out for Lilith. He wanted to tell her about things that he suddenly remembered again—the camel market, the fish market in Ataba Square, the smell of violets in old Garden City—but she didn't come. No one had told him that Lilith had been lying in a white hospital bed for the last three days and that she could no longer move at all. She lay in her bed and said to the people standing around her, "Open the window." Longing blew in with the breeze that carried the smell of guava and wild mulberry and of the mastic and tamarind trees in the garden of an old house by the river, a house with a balcony smothered in gorgeous jasmine and violet and bougainvillea bushes.

She sits in a rocking chair, a small laughing child dressed in white on her lap. An elegantly dressed man smiles at them between sips of clove tea. He smokes his five o'clock cigarette before getting up to prune the branches of the jasmine bush and twine them around taut strings so that they will grow upward and cover the roof of the small villa. He is a man who likes things to be tasteful and ordered and pleasing to the eye.

Lilith closed her eyes and left. She had never watched the little boy curled up against her breast grow into a handsome young man with a wife and a retinue of dignified associates from the Muslim community in Brooklyn. They all stood by him during his mother's illness, an illness that was already in its last stages when the doctor took him aside. "She's very fragile and her memory is completely gone. She might not be able to understand what's going on around her any more. I doubt she has much longer to live." Omar Azzam shakes his head in grief and goes back to reading his Quran. He sits at the open window and gazes at Lilith's pale face. He bends down and uncovers her legs to rub ointment into the ulcers. He contemplates the color of her skin, the marks left by childbirth on her belly, the blemishes on her face, the breast at which he never nursed. The fragrance of the lemon and orange trees in the garden of the Helwan house fills his nostrils, that fragrance that bursts forth when the delicate white blossoms carpet the ground, and he hears the buzzing of bees and sees the ghost of a young woman absorbed in a sketch of a weeping child.

As Lilith's health deteriorated, Nazahat's presence became essential. She was the one who changed the bedpans and took care of Lilith's body lying submissive in the face of approaching death. She turned her over this way and that to avoid putting any pressure on the bed ulcers that had left pitiful marks on every part of her body. Nazahat took her blood pressure and examined her urine while Erica discussed with Abd al-Karim the protocols of washing and shrouding the corpse according to Islamic law. Omar held on tightly to his Quran and reread all the verses about the living and the dead as he watched his childhood pass before his eyes.

Three days later Lilith closed her eyes forever. The wind of long-ing rattled the glass windows and swept in. It whispered to her soul and carried it far away. She went alone, as she had come. The fam-ily and friends who had gathered around her sickbed now bustled about preparing for the burial. Abd al-Karim came with a hearse, Nazahat quickly sewed up the white shroud, and Lilith's son Omar went off to take care of the necessary documents for the burial in the Muslim cemetery in New Jersey. Then, after everyone had per-formed their respective duties, they all went home and picked up the thread of their busy lives.

Hend and Emilia were walking along Fourth Avenue when they ran into Dawij, the girl from Haiti who cleaned houses in the neighborhood. She was too busy to stop and chat but she briefly told them that she was packing up the contents of an old lady's apartment. The lady was called Lilith and she had died a few days ago. Dawij had been hired to pack everything up into cartons and put them out on the sidewalk with a sign that said, *Take me if you want*. "The garbage trucks will take the rest away later," she said.

Music lovers picked up a few of the Liza Minnelli and Frank Sina-tra records and ignored those of Fathiya Ahmad and Layla Murad. Some people rummaged around in the boxes full of silky dresses with plunging necklines like the ones Marilyn Monroe and Sophia Loren used to wear. They inspected the satin robes, the bedspreads and sheets and pillows with Arab and Afghan and Persian-style embroidery, the Indian saris and the old-fashioned handbags. Emilia stood there with her cart, then quickly swooped down on the feast of shoes with a practiced eye. She knew exactly what she wanted and why. She searched for seventies-style platform shoes; pointy, high-heeled shoes like the ones in erotic movies; battered old shoes and others that no one had ever worn; cheap shoes and shoes by famous designers.

Hend poked around in the book cartons. There were a lot of Arabic books in rare editions—*The Arabian Nights* and *The Book of Songs*, *The Prophet* by Khalil Gibran and books of Persian poetry, books that Lilith had handled and read and annotated in the margins. She turned to the cartons containing pillows and bedspreads and exquisitely embroidered sheets, then to the glassware and dresses. "I feel like I know these things," she said to Emilia, "the gilded blue glass sherbet set . . . my mother had one exactly like it in her trousseau. You see this tulip china set? I swear there was one exactly like it in the silver cabinet in my grandmother al-Sharifa's house, God rest her soul. And this chiffon dress . . . I've seen my mother wearing its twin in a photo. I wish I could show it to you." Emilia, who was busy sorting out shoes before the garbage trucks came, laughed shrilly. "The dead lady must have been from an Arab country—and rich!" Two Russian women passed by and exchanged greetings with Emilia. One of them picked up a wig from the pile of cartons. They walked away quickly as one of them said to the other, "You can find so many little things for free in this city—but unfortunately the apartments are too small." Many of the passersby stopped to admire the paintings stacked in wooden crates. The same scene repeated itself for the next couple of days and people came back again and again to carry off things that they really didn't have room for in their homes. Professional antique dealers hauled away the rarest and most unique pieces.

Hend plants herself next to a box stuffed with the papers of a woman she only knew from afar, a woman whose body now lies in a freshly dug grave. She goes through the papers and finds diaries and old photos. She says to Emilia sorrowfully, "Why are they throwing all this stuff out right away? Doesn't she have relatives?" Emilia sighs. "Maybe she doesn't have any kids, dear. And even if she did, where would they put all this old stuff?" Hend examines the signature on dozens of self-portraits in oil and charcoal. "Look, Emilia, this is what Lilith looked like when she was young. Doesn't she look a little like me? Isn't that old scar under her eyebrow like the one I have? Look. . . ."

"All Arabs look alike, dear—I can't tell them apart, to tell you the truth."

Hend stretches out her legs on the sidewalk and leafs through the bits of paper tucked away in the handbags of the woman she would see sitting with Naguib al-Khalili from a distance, a woman whom she sees clearly now for the first time. She goes through all the clippings and letters and photos: Lilith, exposed to the gaze of casual passersby. She stares at the photos of the ubiquitous Omar Azzam—the photos they had sent to Lilith from Cairo so that she could see him growing up thousands of miles away. Each photo was dated on the back *(Cairo, 1975, Mama I miss you, your son Omar)*.

Hend's head spins. She looks at the photograph of a boy who is the same age as her son is now. "Look, Emilia, doesn't this boy look like my son?"

Emilia has no time to look at anything. "Children all look the same at first, then they shoot up and you just can't keep up with all the changes they go through," she grumbles.

Hend lowers her head. Her dizziness gets worse suddenly and a feeling of déjà vu sweeps over her. "Emilia, I know these papers. . . ." And I know that I've written every word in them myself, she thinks. This is my handwriting, they belong to me.

"They're yours now, little one. The lady who wrote them is deader than a doornail and it's all yours now. You can take them and believe whatever you want to believe."

Hend's voice grows more querulous. "You don't understand. I feel like I've lived all this before, that these letters are mine, these words are mine."

Emilia just wants to finish loading up her cart and go because it's starting to get dark. She has no time for this pointless discussion, so to cut the conversation short she says, "You're still young, daughter, you haven't lived anything yet. When you get to be my age you'll realize that everything starts to look and feel the same when you're old. At my age everything that happens feels as though it's happened before. I know I'm getting senile, but you're still young."

She sits on the sidewalk of Fourth Avenue in the middle of the boxes and furniture and lights a cigarette. She can smell the hateful

181

odor of the milk that still burns in her breasts. She clutches a sheaf of papers to her chest, despairing of ever understanding what Lilith wanted to say. Hend walks next to Emilia as she drags her cart loaded with shoes behind her. The old Russian woman's face suddenly starts to take on Grandmother Zaynab's features before Hend's eyes—the deep wrinkles, the single tooth and flaming red irises—and Hend hears the echoing rustle of the rabbits scurrying out of their lairs and surreptitiously devouring the piles of vegetable scraps.

Emilia moves away down the street, hunched over like a weird apparition. Her parting words linger in the air between them. "You mustn't get too worked up about these things . . . such is the way of the world . . . everything gets mixed up suddenly. We believe what we want to believe, then amnesia strikes and you don't even know who you are—or used to be—any more. We all become sorry copies of each other in the end. But you're still too young. You're too young to forget, my little one."

Hend hurries down the sidewalk toward her house. She runs to escape Emilia's terrifying face. She does what she used to do when she was a child: she buries her head under the covers and tries to blot out her fear. In the dream that comes, the legions of identical little rabbits peep out of their lairs and scurry up the pile of clover in her father's courtyard. They nibble furiously on the green leaves, then dash back to their dark maze of tunnels under the ground of the pantry room. The old women used to say that rabbits come up from their subterranean lairs to watch over the dead, that they roam the underworld eternally, reproducing themselves in the twilight space between life and death. Hend hears the hesitant patter of their nimble feet in her dreams. She stuffs a handful of hair into her mouth and reaches down to feel her underpants under the covers, wet with fear.

Modern Arabic Literature
from the American University in Cairo Press

Bahaa Abdelmegid *Saint Theresa* and *Sleeping with Strangers*
Ibrahim Abdel Meguid *Birds of Amber* • *Distant Train*
No One Sleeps in Alexandria • *The Other Place*
Yahya Taher Abdullah *The Collar and the Bracelet* • *The Mountain of Green Tea*
Leila Abouzeid *The Last Chapter*
Hamdi Abu Golayyel *A Dog with No Tail* • *Thieves in Retirement*
Yusuf Abu Rayya *Wedding Night*
Ahmed Alaidy *Being Abbas el Abd*
Idris Ali *Dongola* • *Poor*
Rasha al Ameer *Judgment Day*
Radwa Ashour *Granada* • *Specters*
Ibrahim Aslan *The Heron* • *Nile Sparrows*
Alaa Al Aswany *Chicago* • *Friendly Fire* • *The Yacoubian Building*
Fadi Azzam *Sarmada*
Fadhil al-Azzawi *Cell Block Five* • *The Last of the Angels* • *The Traveler and the Innkeeper*
Ali Bader *Papa Sartre*
Liana Badr *The Eye of the Mirror*
Hala El Badry *A Certain Woman* • *Muntaha*
Salwa Bakr *The Golden Chariot* • *The Man from Bashmour* • *The Wiles of Men*
Halim Barakat *The Crane*
Hoda Barakat *Disciples of Passion* • *The Tiller of Waters*
Mourid Barghouti *I Saw Ramallah* • *I Was Born There, I Was Born Here*
Mohamed Berrada *Like a Summer Never to Be Repeated*
Mohamed El-Bisatie *Clamor of the Lake* • *Drumbeat* • *Hunger* • *Over the Bridge*
Mahmoud Darwish *The Butterfly's Burden*
Tarek Eltayeb *Cities without Palms* • *The Palm House*
Mansoura Ez Eldin *Maryam's Maze*
Ibrahim Farghali *The Smiles of the Saints*
Hamdy el-Gazzar *Black Magic*
Randa Ghazy *Dreaming of Palestine*
Gamal al-Ghitani *Pyramid Texts* • *The Zafarani Files* • *Zayni Barakat*
Tawfiq al-Hakim *The Essential Tawfiq al-Hakim*
Yahya Hakki *The Lamp of Umm Hashim*
Abdelilah Hamdouchi *The Final Bet*
Bensalem Himmich *The Polymath* • *The Theocrat*
Taha Hussein *The Days*
Sonallah Ibrahim *Cairo: From Edge to Edge* • *The Committee* • *Zaat*
Yusuf Idris *City of Love and Ashes* • *The Essential Yusuf Idris*
Denys Johnson-Davies *The AUC Press Book of Modern Arabic Literature* • *Homecoming*
In a Fertile Desert • *Under the Naked Sky*
Said al-Kafrawi *The Hill of Gypsies*
Mai Khaled *The Magic of Turquoise*
Sahar Khalifeh *The End of Spring*
The Image, the Icon and the Covenant • *The Inheritance*
Edwar al-Kharrat *Rama and the Dragon* • *Stones of Bobello*

Betool Khedairi *Absent*
Mohammed Khudayyir *Basrayatha*
Ibrahim al-Koni *Anubis* • *Gold Dust* • *The Puppet* • *The Seven Veils of Seth*
Naguib Mahfouz *Adrift on the Nile* • *Akhenaten: Dweller in Truth*
Arabian Nights and Days • *Autumn Quail* • *Before the Throne* • *The Beggar*
The Beginning and the End • *Cairo Modern* • *The Cairo Trilogy: Palace Walk*
Palace of Desire • *Sugar Street* • *Children of the Alley* • *The Coffeehouse*
The Day the Leader Was Killed • *The Dreams* • *Dreams of Departure*
Echoes of an Autobiography • *The Essential Naguib Mahfouz* • *The Final Hour*
The Harafish • *Heart of the Night* • *In the Time of Love*
The Journey of Ibn Fattouma • *Karnak-Cafe* • *Khan al-Khalili* • *Khufu's Wisdom*
Life's Wisdom • *Love in the Rain* • *Midaq Alley* • *The Mirage* • *Miramar* • *Mirrors*
Morning and Evening Talk • *Naguib Mahfouz at Sidi Gaber* • *Respected Sir*
Rhadopis of Nubia • *The Search* • *The Seventh Heaven* • *Thebes at War*
The Thief and the Dogs • *The Time and the Place* • *Voices from the Other World*
Wedding Song • *The Wisdom of Naguib Mahfouz*
Mohamed Makhzangi *Memories of a Meltdown*
Alia Mamdouh *The Loved Ones* • *Naphtalene*
Selim Matar *The Woman of the Flask*
Ibrahim al-Mazini *Ten Again*
Yousef Al-Mohaimeed *Munira's Bottle* • *Wolves of the Crescent Moon*
Hassouna Mosbahi *A Tunisian Tale*
Ahlam Mosteghanemi *Chaos of the Senses* • *Memory in the Flesh*
Shakir Mustafa *Contemporary Iraqi Fiction: An Anthology*
Mohamed Mustagab *Tales from Dayrut*
Buthaina Al Nasiri *Final Night*
Ibrahim Nasrallah *Inside the Night* • *Time of White Horses*
Haggag Hassan Oddoul *Nights of Musk*
Mona Prince *So You May See*
Mohamed Mansi Qandil *Moon over Samarqand*
Abd al-Hakim Qasim *Rites of Assent*
Somaya Ramadan *Leaves of Narcissus*
Mekkawi Said *Cairo Swan Song*
Ghada Samman *The Night of the First Billion*
Mahdi Issa al-Saqr *East Winds, West Winds*
Rafik Schami *The Calligrapher's Secret* • *Damascus Nights*
The Dark Side of Love
Habib Selmi *The Scents of Marie-Claire*
Khairy Shalaby *The Hashish Waiter* • *The Lodging House*
The Time-Travels of the Man Who Sold Pickles and Sweets
Miral al-Tahawy *Blue Aubergine* • *Brooklyn Heights* • *Gazelle Tracks* • *The Tent*
Bahaa Taher *As Doha Said* • *Love in Exile*
Fuad al-Takarli *The Long Way Back*
Zakaria Tamer *The Hedgehog*
M. M. Tawfik *Murder in the Tower of Happiness*
Mahmoud Al-Wardani *Heads Ripe for Plucking*
Amina Zaydan *Red Wine*
Latifa al-Zayyat *The Open Door*